MORTE À DELI

MORTE
À
DELI

Christine Cook

Porch Swing Press
ANN ARBOR, MICHIGAN

For more information please write:
Porch Swing Press
2258 Courtney Circle Court
Ann Arbor, MI 48103.

Library of Congress Cataloging in Publication Data

Cook, Christine
        Morte À Deli

        1. Mystery.   2. Fiction
I. Title

ISBN 0-9724166-0-9

Ordering information is located on the back page of the book.

Morte À Deli, First Edition 10 9 8 7 6 5 4 3 2 1

Dedicated to my father, Theodore Charney.
Without his support, I would never have
had the courage to write.
And to my husband and beloved children:
I could not do this without your support.

Contents

1   "Fly in the Ointment" 9
2   "Deli Dilemma" 16
3   "Guns and Butter" 20
4   "A Hankering to Investigate" 25
5   "Checking Out the Competition" 30
6   "Out on the Town" 37
7   "Light on the Case" 44
8   "Death by Potato Salad" 51
9   "Panic Sets In" 59
10   "A Big Mistake on my Part" 65
11   "An Unexpected Day Off" 76
12   "Other People's Help" 85
13   "Suspect #1—Me" 93
14   "Journalists of the World Unite" 99
15   "Mourning in the Morning" 104
16   "D'Arcy Carter, Hacker Extraordinaire" 109
17   "A Nasty Thought" 112
18   "A Possible Buyer" 121
19   "Joe Shows his True Colors" 127
20   "Lifting Names" 136
21   "What Salad is This?" 142
22   "Down for the Count" 148
23   "Meeting the Motorcycle Gang" 155
24   "More than One Investigator" 158
25   "Building up the Case" 165
26   "Getting a Grilling" 171
27   "Watched Like a Hawk" 181
28   "Father Confessor" 188
29   "Turning a Stone Over Again" 194
30   "A Puzzle Piece Fits" 199
31   "Closing In" 204
32   "A Cut Above" 212
33   "Dressing for Murder" 215
34   "All Wrapped Up" 221

CHAPTER 1
"Fly in the Ointment"

I woke to a hammer above my head. I looked at the LED on my clock. 7 a.m. "Peyton, what the hell are you doing?" I yelled as I pulled back the covers and swung my feet over the side of the bed.

He didn't answer. I groaned, and grabbed my robe. I'd planned to sleep until nine. I had an interview today at a private investigator's office, and I didn't want to blow it. I got cranky when I didn't get at least eight hours of sleep. Peyton was going to die.

"Peyton, God dammit!" I screamed. I ran up the stairs two at a time. "Do you have to wake me up at seven?"

When I reached the attic, I stopped. Peyton stood up. A hammer hung limply at his side. "It's July second," he said. "I told you a month ago I'd renovate the second floor for you. Don't you want me to do it anymore? I've got great plans. First, I'm going to lay down the floor. To do that, I've got to pull out these panelled areas. I'll double joist the floor in a few spots, lay carpet down. Burgundy would be nice, don't you think? But first, we'll hinge the roof—"

"Excuse me?"

"Hinge the roof. Take the line of the back roof, raise it three and a half feet. Add three feet to the upstairs, the whole length of the house."

"That's nice. But I can't afford to hinge the roof of my house. How are we going to get that kind of money when I don't even have a job yet?"

"Oh, ye of little faith." Peyton is a tall muscular black man. When I heard him say that, I had to laugh. I hadn't expected archaic English to come from his mouth. But I knew he was right.

Peyton has created miracles in my home since he moved in two years ago. Peyton's an Interior Design major at Eastern Michigan University. He could furnish a six thousand square foot house elegantly for a grand, I swear. So far, he's redecorated my living room five times, plus my dining room, bedroom, and bathroom; all for less than three hundred dollars. If anyone could build my upstairs for me and do it on my budget, Peyton could.

I own a tiny Cape Cod with a finished first floor and an unfinished second floor. The only reason I could buy it in the first place was that it was on terrible real estate at the end of one of Detroit Metro Airport's runways.

I had nine hundred square feet of usable living space, but Peyton and I recently agreed I should up the resale value of my home by developing the upstairs into an open concept bedroom-bathroom suite with a small loft office.

This diversion on Peyton's part did not answer my question. "Yes, but do you have to begin our project at seven o'clock in the morning?" Before Peyton could reply, the doorbell rang. "What the hell is going on today?" I asked, and ran back down the stairs.

Standing at my doorstep was Sid Field. Sid was a co-owner of the Nouveau Deli, a restaurant I had worked at, but recently quit. Sid was a jovial guy, easy going and even-tempered. He was the only manager I'd really enjoyed working for. He was very tall, with a full head of brown hair and the body of an out of shape football player.

He looked very serious there on my welcome mat. Was that worry I saw in his eyes? It might have been the first time I'd ever seen him upset. I invited him in. "What's up, Sid? Want some coffee? I just got up."

"Yes, thanks, I would. Hope I didn't wake you." He licked his lips, then patted them dry with the back of his hand. I'd truly never seen him look so nervous. Usually, he was the kind of guy who rolled easily through crises. I wondered for a moment if he wanted me to come back to work. Not that I'd go if he did. But that wouldn't explain the nervousness.

"Sit down," I said, and indicated the black and white barber-striped couch. "I'll be right back."

Peyton had made coffee before he went upstairs, so it was ready for me when I walked into the kitchen. I filled two mugs, then turned off the switch on the coffee maker. In one mug, I added skim milk. In the other, I added the cream Peyton had bought, plus four teaspoons of sugar. I went back to the living room, and handed Sid the sugary coffee.

After he tasted it, he asked, "How did you know I like my coffee this way?"

I laughed. "Every morning for a year, I watched you fix your coffee. How else would I know?"

"That's just the kind of details I need you to notice."

I had raised my coffee to my lips, but I stopped. "What?" No answer to my question was forthcoming, so I went ahead and sipped. The coffee was hot. It burned my lips. I touched them lightly to cool them down.

Sid looked embarrassed. He stared down, and I hoped there were no dust mice crawling around on the hardwood floor. As though he had read my mind, he looked up and checked the rest of the room out. "You've got a really nice place here."

"Thank you." I was proud of my house. Peyton had deco-

rated the whole place with a theme of black, white, and prima-
ries. The living room had black and white striped upholstery
on the couch and two over-stuffed chairs, which sat on a black
and white zebra patterned shag rug, surrounded by lemony yellow walls.

That's all he had seen so far. Maybe Sid would want to
tour the rest of the house, and thereby further procrastinate on
telling me why he was really here.

Instead, he said, "A friend of mine suggested I talk to
you. He thought you might be able to help me, and you'd be
discreet."

"Who?"

"Bill Noble."

"Lieutenant Colonel Noble?" This surprised me. I had
no idea Sid knew LTC Noble. It made me realize just how
small this world really was. I'd met the man myself a few
weeks ago, in a place so far from the deli I would never have
considered that he and Sid knew each other. He'd been in Grayling when I became embroiled with an illegal environmental
waste dump which was on Army property.

Noble was the Environmental Liaison officer for the
Michigan Army National Guard. He'd hired me to find out
who had dumped waste there. That had been my first unoffi-
cial case in a career I hoped to pursue. A career that might be
the first of fourteen jobs I really enjoyed. One I might actually,
finally, succeed at. "How do you know Colonel Noble?"

Sid waved his hand as though he had already dismissed
the question. "Oh, we went to school together."

"What'd he tell you about me that you didn't know when
I worked at the deli?"

"He seems to think you could help me with a little investigation I have." He cleared his throat and paused yet again. I
really wanted him to get to the point.

"Investigation?" I put my coffee cup down on the table
and leaned forward, my elbows on my knees. "What kind of
investigation?"

I became aware that Sid's right knee was bouncing up and down. His coffee mug jiggled, dangerously close to being spilled. I wanted him to put the mug down before he spattered coffee on the carpet. I opened my mouth, but suddenly his knee stopped its dance. He cleared his throat again. "Uh—I seem to think, well, it's just that—"

"Sid, spit it out, you're driving me crazy!"

"One of my employees came to me last week. Told me he thought he'd gotten food poisoning."

"At Nouveau Deli?" I said incredulously. Sid nodded. "How on earth would that happen?"

"He had some salmon salad a week or so ago. He said it tasted close to the edge, even though he'd made it just a few hours before, out of brand new salmon. But, six hours later, he was vomiting and had a fever, just like salmonella, if you'll pardon the pun. He was sick two days."

The story seemed strange. If the salad had been properly stored, it would have been refrigerated since the minute it was made. If there's one thing I had learned at Nouveau Deli, it was the importance of good sanitation. They drummed it into us from the first day of work how to avoid salmonella and staph contamination.

If I'd let a salad sit for more than five minutes before I put it in the refrigerator, I'd get chewed out. If I didn't get my bleach bucket changed exactly every two hours, someone would see it and be on my ass about it. Having someone down with food poisoning was totally unthinkable.

"That's not possible."

"I wish that were true. If it were an isolated incident, I'd think the guy ate somewhere else, got sick and blamed it on us. But he knows what he's doing, and I hate to say it, I have reason to believe it's not the first time. A lot of food's been going bad before its time. I think we're being sabotaged."

Out of his breast pocket, he pulled a folded piece of paper, which, with shaky hands, he smoothed on his knee. Then he handed it to me.

I took it. It was an 8"x11" piece of paper, a rollup of the food loss for the week. "This, I assume, is a week of food thrown out because it's gone bad or been dropped."

"Only the food that's gone bad." He took a big swig of coffee. His knee had started its tattoo again.

I looked down at the sheet. Mom's potato salad, fifteen pounds; Nouveau potato salad, ten pounds; goat cheese and pinto pasta, ten pounds, then another fifteen pounds. In all, a total of $1200 worth of salads had been thrown out. "Is this a normal food loss sheet for a week?"

"I should say not, d'Arcy," he said. "If that were normal, we would have been out of business five years ago. But it's somehow, suddenly, becoming par for the course. We've tried to institute procedures to lower our waste, and it seems to be getting worse instead of better."

I remembered those procedures. They'd been legendary, and had caused more than a few of the supervisors anger and frustration. Me included. Procedures like those went against the insistence on quality that the deli supposedly upheld.

In my mouth, I could almost taste the fizziness of a salad gone bad. We had to taste each salad at the beginning of our supervisor shift. During slow weeks, in January or February, a salad would go bad every other day or so. After a while, I could tell by sight when a meat salad had gone bad. The oil on the top of the mayonnaise would create a rainbow along the top of the pan.

Normally, we'd write it up as a loss, and throw out the salad. The deli's waste reduction program insisted that we attempt to sell the salads before they went bad. A good idea on the surface, except we'd been doing that all along. Every bit of salad we had to throw out threatened to affect our paycheck.

"But sabotage, Sid? Why do you think it's sabotage?"

"That's what I want to hire you to find out. It could be an external or internal job. I just don't know."

I laughed. "I'm not for 'hire,' as you put it. I'm not a legal private eye. I have no training, I have no license. Find someone who's trained to do this."

"But you're trained as something more important to me. You've already trained as a supervisor for the restaurant. You can go back to work and no one would suspect you to be the investigating person."

"Whoa! Hoo!" Peyton was yelling upstairs. I could hear him clatter down the steps behind Sid's head. The door to the stairs opened and closed. Peyton jumped into the living room. "Look what I—"

He spotted Sid. "Oh, I'm sorry. I just assumed you were a Jehovah's Witness or something, and you'd be gone by now." He looked at me, confused but with a look like he couldn't wait to tell me something. "I'll talk to you later." He went out of the room, and into his bedroom. He closed the door behind him.

After he left, I was silent for a few minutes. Finally, I said, "Look, Sid, I'm not trained to be a private investigator. I don't know what Colonel Noble told you, but—"

"I'm not looking for an expert investigator. You'll fit right in, and you'll know when someone's not doing something properly. Come on, d'Arcy, I need you to do this before a customer gets sick and decides to sue."

I lay back in my chair and covered my eyes with my hands. I rubbed the sockets with my palms. I wanted to quell the headache before it started. "Oh, God, Sid," I sighed. "I never wanted to go back to the deli. I've really enjoyed my month away."

He cleared his throat. "There's something else I think you should know before you say you won't do it."

I pulled my hands away from my face and looked at him. He looked back at me, his brown eyes bulging in his face. I nodded to tell him to go on.

"This is really hard for me to say."

"Yeah, that's why you've been avoiding it till now. Out with it."

His eyes lowered, as though he couldn't bear to look at me. "I think there may be murder involved."

CHAPTER 2
"Deli Dilemma"

This announcement made me sit up straight in my chair. "What?"

"One of Lynnette's friends recently died, of a stomach flu virus. At least, that's what we thought it was at the time."

"And you think it wasn't."

"Well, I know he ate at the restaurant the day before he got sick."

I could feel my blood pressure rise. "Sid, are you crazy? That's, that's way out of my league. I'm not even a private eye, and you want me to investigate a homicide."

"You did it for Bill Noble."

"That was different. What you need to do is contact the police."

His face went white. "No, that's the worst thing I could do. Don't you understand? Right now, they don't know anything about this. But if they find out, they'll contact the Health Department. D'Arcy, they could close me down. I'd be ruined. Please, you have to help me."

I shouldn't accept it, I told myself. What would the investigative firm I was interviewing with today think of this? I could get in real trouble. I had no idea what I was doing.

I sat back in my chair. Sid raised his face to look at me. He had a pleasant face, but a face etched with pain and worry. It was a face that was hard to say "no" to. Much as it went against my grain to do this, I said, "You pay me twenty five an hour, and I'll think about it."

His mouth closed. He licked his lips and rubbed his palms against his faded blue jeans. He turned red. I went on. "Including hours I'm not on the line, but doing background checks and research."

"Twenty five dollars?" He asked. He gulped at the air. "That seems high."

Why was I playing hardball? Because Sid needed to remember the seriousness of the situation, that's why. "Of course it seems high. How much do you spend at your highest hourly rate there? Six, seven dollars? But let me ask you this: What's your salary, Sid? As owner of the deli." He cleared his throat, and I laughed. "C'mon, Sid, $25 an hour is child's pay for a P.I. Many of them make over three hundred a day. And this is murder we're talking about, here."

"I don't know."

I stood up. "Well, then I'll see you later."

"Wait—okay, I'm sorry. Sit down. We'll talk."

I sat down.

"How 'bout twenty an hour?"

"You don't seem to understand. Twenty five dollars an hour is my only offer." I figured if he didn't agree to twenty five, I wouldn't have to work on this case. I would much rather start my investigative career legally, under a registered P.I., and not at the deli I'd just escaped from. And I was too much of a novice for a possible homicide.

Sid stroked his chin. "Okay."

"I'll draw up a contract for you."

Sid nodded, but he didn't like it. He frowned. "I'll pay you out of my own pocket; the difference between your old hourly rate and the twenty five, that is. That way the payroll office won't question what you're making."

I nodded. "So tell me what you think is going on." I leaned back in my chair. "For example, you said the employee who complained of food poisoning, he ate the salmon salad. The one with yogurt and sour cream and pieces of lox?"

"Yes."

"What did your friend eat when he came in? Also salmon salad?"

For a second, I thought Sid almost bristled. Then he relaxed and said, "You mean Lynnette's friend. No, as I recall, he had one of the potato salads. The one with hard boiled eggs in a cream and mayonnaise base."

I nodded, stood up and found of pen and paper. "What was his name?"

"Ben. Benjamin Mitchell."

I took a few notes. "Any ideas who might want to sabotage you?"

"Well, personally, I think it's the new bakeshop down the street, Joe's, you know which one I mean?"

I nodded. Joe's had opened three years ago, and immediately had started trying to take Nouveau Deli's clientele away. Joe's marketing department, such as it was, attempted to downgrade the Nouveau Deli's quality and service abilities. The campaign had had little if any effect, as far as I could tell.

I could see what Sid meant, though. If word got out that Nouveau Deli was having a sanitation or possible health problem, sales would probably go down, and Joe's stood to gain.

Worse yet, if the Health Department found out, the restaurant would have a full scale investigation, with the possible result of closing Nouveau Deli down. Heaven only knew what would happen if someone sued the deli, as Sid feared. I could see why he was so nervous.

"If you think it's Joe's, have you talked to them about it?"

"Hell, no. I'd be feeding right into his hands. Why give them the chance to publicize? No, we have to catch them in the act."

I raised my hands involuntarily, then lowered them. "But, Sid, it's a possible murder."

"And only a possible murder. I'm not going to do something that will threaten my business, and then find out it wasn't related in any way. That's why I need your help." Nervously, he ran his fingers through his hair.

"Okay, okay. So, do you think you have a double agent kind of thing going on? Someone who works for Joe and for you?"

"Hmm. I never thought of that. Good point."

He stood up. "Anything else you can think of that you need, call me. Oh, and please, only speak to me about this matter. The less people know about the problem, the better."

I got up, too. "Understood."

"Jennifer will call you with your schedule over the weekend. She'll be thrilled to have you back." We shook hands. "Thanks a lot for your help."

We said our goodbyes, and I watched him walk to his car. When he was safely in the beige Caddy and I had closed the door, I leaned against it. I felt terrified and euphoric at the same time. Terrified that I should start out investigating sabotage and/or murder without the safety net of a P.I. license. Euphoric that I had actually gotten him to agree to twenty five dollars an hour. I hoped it wouldn't get me in trouble during my interview today.

CHAPTER 3
"Guns and Butter"

Peyton came running out from his room. "What what what?"

I explained the situation to him, and Peyton's eyes lit up. "Think of all the fun fixes we can do upstairs with that kind of money."

"Now, Peyton, that's not the agreement, and you know it." Peyton's decorating had been in lieu of rent for the last two years. Granted, this project would cost us more than the normal $150 per month, but I felt like giving him a hard time.

"I know, honey, I know. But, not to steal your thunder, you understand, but I have got to show you something."

Whatever it was he'd found must have been good. If it were bad, he wouldn't be nearly jumping up and down. He opened the door to the upstairs. He picked up the cat and tossed her to the living room so she wouldn't get up there and hurt herself. She mewed angrily, and crouched into a pounce position.

"Honey!" Peyton said. He'd added an extra syllable to the word. "You ain't gonna believe this!"

I knew when he laid his Southern accent on thick that Peyton was truly excited. He bounded the stairs three at a time. I followed him up.

"You ever seen the stuff behind that?" he asked, and pointed to the temporary pine panelling on the back wall, which probably had been put up shortly after the house was built in the 1940s.

I shook my head. "There's no entrance into that part of the house. What'd you find?"

Peyton put his hand into the hole he'd made in the panelling, and pulled out a shotgun. All at once, I saw a glimmer of fear from my past, then it was gone. I stepped back, knocking my butt against the banister. "Holy shit, Peyton."

"It's okay, d'Arcy, there's no ammo in any of them. I checked."

"How many are there?"

"Ten."

"Ten? And they've been here all along?"

"Probably." He pulled out each stock, and lay them down with great respect. "These guns must all date from well before World War II. This one here's a Browning Over/Under shotgun, worth maybe some major bucks. I think they're all probably worth something."

The last one he pulled out gleamed. The barrel had been polished to a soft sheen, and every grain of the gorgeous wood stood out, as though it were a three dimensional picture. It almost looked like a plastic replica. I had never seen such glorious depth in wood before.

"My daddy would have loved this rifle," he said. "If you bought one like this now, it would be several thousand dollars. I don't know what a period piece like this would go for."

I looked at the rifles for awhile. Ten rifles, all of which looked like collector's items. "It looks like the renovation might pay for itself. We need to find out what these are worth."

"Aye-aye ma'am. I'll get right on it."

I looked at my watch. "9:30, already? Where'd the last two hours go?" I ran downstairs to the bathroom to start my dressing routine. I had to look good today, since I had a job interview with a private investigator at 10:30.

After I got back from Grayling a few weeks before, I had taken the comments of a certain attractive lawyer named Tim Reams to heart. He told me I should look into becoming a P.I., after my work on a mystery up North. If I'd been a detective, I probably would have called it a "case."

I had no background in investigation, and frankly had never considered getting into this line of work. I had a degree in Biology with a specialty in Animal Behavior, but I'd never worked in my field.

Instead, I'd bounced from job to job, sticking mainly in the teaching and restaurant fields. Fourteen jobs later, I went through an early mid-life crisis. What did I really want to do with my life?

Just about this time, I got involved in the mystery in Grayling, and discovered I liked solving it.

Now, I was investigating possible opportunities in the field. When I cleaned out my deceased aunt's house in Ann Arbor not long ago, I went to the library to find out what I needed to become a licensed private investigator. It turned out I needed to apprentice with a detective for a few years before I could get a license. I hoped the private eye I had an appointment with today would invite me to join his firm.

I washed my hair and blow-dried it straight, then pulled it back into a reverse french braid. I put on some makeup, too, and then put on the clothes I'd laid out the night before.

Since it was July, I'd figured it would be hot as hell, so I had chosen my cream colored interview suit, made of tropical weight wool. It was six years old, but I'd chosen a classic single button jacket and straight skirt, so it didn't look out of style, at least to me. I put a white short-sleeved cotton shirt underneath, and wore fresh water pearls and a choker. I thought I looked pretty good.

Peyton had promised me the use of his car, since he planned to work upstairs the whole day. Thank God for small miracles. I could just see it, all dressed up in my suit, riding my bicycle down Middle Belt Road. That's another drawback to bikes. You can't get dressed up for work, because you'll still look like crap when you get there.

I supposed soon I'd have to break down and buy a car. Maybe a clunker, or better yet, a little Japanese thing, and really get my dad riled up. He's a retired vice president from GM, and we haven't gotten along in a long time. Personally, I think it's stubbornness on my part and stupidity on his, but of course, I'm biased.

I was headed out the door when the phone rang. I was going to let Peyton pick it up, but then decided against it. It might be Ralph Hughes, the guy I was on my way to see. "Hello?"

"May I speak to d'Arcy Carter?"

The voice was familiar. "This is she."

"Tim Reams. How are you?"

I felt a tingle of excitement go down my spine. "Hi. Terrific. How about you?"

"Good. Hey, I heard some interesting news about that deli you used to work in today. I'm really glad you aren't working there any longer."

"Oh, what have you heard?"

"Well, I can't say. Just suffice it to say, it doesn't look good for the deli."

Uh oh, maybe this was the potential lawsuit Sid was trying to head off. But Tim was a corporate lawyer. How would he know about a civil suit? "What is it, are they being sued?"

"So say, what are you doing this evening?"

He said it to change the subject, and I appreciated the fact that he had remained confidential. It took me a minute to realize I should reply to his question.

"Nothing in particular. Why?"

"I've got tickets to the Detroit Opera. Would you like to go with me?"

"Sure." I couldn't find my heartbeat for a moment, and I thought maybe I'd just died. Then I could feel it, vibrating in my chest. "What's playing?"

"The Student Prince."

"Great. That's supposed to be one of the funny ones, right?"

"Beats me."

I laughed at his answer, and he laughed with me.

We agreed on a time to meet. He'd pick me up and take me to the Whitney for a pre-theater dinner.

"See you later," I said. I tried to keep any excess excitement out of my voice. This was my first date in almost three years.

CHAPTER 4
"A Hankering to Investigate"

Ralph Hughes' office was located just off the corner of Middle Belt and Michigan Avenue. The office was the third section from the left in an unassuming shopping center I'd never really noticed before, housed between a used paperback book store and a Minnesota Fabrics. The glass door had two words on it: Hughes Investigations.

I got out of the car and straightened my skirt. It felt like it was easily 93 degrees outside, and my shirt was sticking to my armpits. My pantyhose were damp the whole length of my thighs. I checked my watch. 10:28. You're a prompt one, d'Arcy, I said to myself, and walked inside.

Here, the air was slightly cooler, as a loud air conditioner struggled to keep the degrees down. In the center of the lobby was a plain walnut veneer desk. A woman roughly fifty years old sat behind it. She had owl-shaped glasses on, and a white shirt with a little blue print that looked like sail boats. She smiled pleasantly and said, "Hello. May I help you?"

"Yes, I have an appointment with Ralph Hughes."

"You do?" She checked the large calendar in front of her. "Oh, you must be d'Arcy Carter, is that right?" I nodded. "Ralph will be back in just a moment. He called from his nine o'clock appointment to say he'd be a bit late. Can you wait?"

"Sure." I sat down and laid my clutch purse in my lap, folded my fingers together, then unfolded them again. I took the chance to look around. The room was cheerful enough. The colors of green and brass abounded, so the lobby looked like a barroom built in the early eighties. A myriad of spider plants hung from the ceiling in macrame planters, and the carpet was the green indoor-outdoor kind. Wood veneer and gold colored accents covered all the furniture. A door, behind the woman's desk, led presumably to the rest of the office.

"There are three of us here," she said, to make conversation while we waited. "There's Ralph and Jeffrey Jenkins. Such a shame about Calico, though."

"Calico?"

"Yes, dear, the cat. She died about a year ago. Couldn't hang on after—Well, it all started when Bart died."

I assumed Bart must have been another cat, and I nodded. "I'd be heartsick if Pantera ever died," I said.

"Pantera's an odd name."

"She's a black cat."

"Oh, do you have a cat, then?"

I nodded again. To my surprise, the woman opened a drawer in her desk and pulled out a piece of knitting. It was white and pink, and looked fairly small. Was business slow? Chances were getting slimmer that I would glean a job from my efforts here. "What's your name?" I asked.

"Genevieve. I'm Ralph's wife. I'm sorry, I should have introduced myself."

"That's okay. What's that you're making?" I stood up, and came over to the desk.

"A sweater. Our daughter's due to have a little girl in a couple of weeks. Do you knit, by any chance?"

I nodded.

"Well, maybe you could help me. I don't quite understand this particular direction. It says 'do double seed stitch for three inches.' But I don't even know how to do single seed stitch."

"Here, I'll show you," I said, and took the needles from her. "You knit two, purl two, the whole way across," I said and demonstrated the stitch for her, "Then come back, knit on top of the purls, purl on the knits, and you get a nubbly stitch like this." I finished the second row and showed it to her.

"My, you're fast. You don't knit like I do. Show me how you do that. You don't throw the yarn at all?"

"I do a Continental stitch, since I just taught myself by looking at pictures in books." I showed her.

"I like you," she said, after we'd discussed knitting for a minute or two longer. She put her knitting away. "Well, coffee break is over. I'll tell you, the work load I've been having recently. See, I do all the billing, and since Bart died. . . .Say, you wouldn't be looking for a job, would you?"

"Well," I said. How should I tell her I really wasn't interested in the receptionist's job she probably meant to offer me? I needn't have worried, though, because as I opened my mouth, the door opened behind me. I stood up from the perch I'd unconsciously taken as I showed Genevieve how to knit. I straightened my skirt, and took the chance to wipe my suddenly clammy hands.

"Are you d'Arcy Carter?" the tall man who'd just walked in asked. He was in his fifties, too, and relatively dapper, I may add. He had a waxed handle-bar mustache, which had gone salt and pepper, and wavy hair that he combed across his head and controlled with some hair goop that smelled like English Leather. He looked more like a college English professor than a modern private investigator. Maybe he was Sherlock Holmes reincarnated.

We shook hands. "I'm sorry I'm so late. Did Genevieve offer you coffee?"

"Oh, dear, I didn't. Will you ever forgive me? Let me get you a mug."

She handed me one, a black floral mug. "You'll find the coffee machine right beyond this door," she said, opening the door behind her desk. "Ralph will be right in, as soon as I give him his messages."

I helped myself to some coffee. Through the door, I watched Ralph and Genevieve, their heads bent together, talking quietly. Were they talking about me? Positive or negative? No, dear, I don't think so. She's a knitter, she likes cats. She'd never make a good private investigator.

After I stirred some powdered non-dairy creamer into my coffee, Ralph came in, and I followed him into the back office. It was one large room, with three desks, identical to the one out front. Ralph led me to the desk in the center, and indicated the leather chair in front of it. I sat down and put my mug on the desktop.

"I do apologize," he said as he sat down. "I've been having to do the work of two men, and I do it all half as well. So, what may I do for you?"

"Well, sir—"

"Stop that right now."

"What?"

"Don't call me sir, my name is Ralph. Go on."

"Well," I paused, "Ralph, I came to speak to you about the field of private investigation. You see, I'm interested in it as a career."

"Why on earth for? It isn't a pretty career to say the least. Not for a woman. I'm not trying to be sexist, you understand. But, especially if, say, you end up doing a homicide investigation."

"I know that, but as far as I can tell, homicide is not the most common form of private investigation. There are a lot of other things one can investigate. Domestic squabbles, for example, or corporate matters."

"Well, you have done your homework, I'll say that. None of it is as glamourous as it's cracked up to be."

I hesitated. "I'm not looking for glamour. I do, though, have some experience, however inept, with homicide." Quickly, I described what happened in Grayling and followed it up with the unfortunate events of a few weeks ago when I found my great aunt had been murdered.

When I finished, Ralph remained quiet. I waited a moment, then rushed on. "You see, I'd like to get into private investigation, but I can't without some kind of apprenticeship first. So I wanted to ask you if you needed someone like me." He looked at me. His brown eyes looked black, and bored into my very being. "I'd be willing to start as low man—"

"Could you be quiet for just a moment and let me think?" He tapped his fingers on the desk blotter. I remained quiet. As usual, I'd blown it. Woman hanged for talking too much.

CHAPTER 5
"Checking Out the Competition"

"Well," he said, and I jumped. "The fact is, I could use some help. Bartholomew, my partner for fifteen years, died last year. Jeffrey and I thought we could do the case load ourselves, but the truth is, we've been getting busier and busier. Right now, he's on vacation. When could you start?"

"Almost immediately," I said. "Oh, wait, that's not quite true." I explained to him the situation I had with Sid and Nouveau Deli.

"You know what you're doing is not legal, charging someone for your services when you don't have a license."

I nodded. I tried to swallow the lump that had gathered just underneath the pendulum in my throat.

"And it's dangerous, too. You'll have to be careful, if that one death really does fit in with the sabotage. But, maybe we can work something out, and you can have this as your first case under me."

I refrained from cheering. I promised myself instead to

put all that enthusiasm into doing a good job, proving I could do this. I just had to do well.

"I don't think Sid will go for any more money an hour than I talked him into."

He winked at me. "We'll work something out. Anything you need from my end?"

"Well, I need to find out more on a guy named Ben Mitchell. He died of the flu a couple weeks ago. But it might not have been the flu. I need to look into it, but I don't know how without stirring up curiosity."

"Okay, I'll try to find out where he lived, maybe track down where he worked, that kind of thing. Will that help?"

"Great, thanks."

As I left the office, Genevieve's voice followed me. "I hope you'll come see us again."

"Oh, I will," I turned and waved, "I will." I walked out of the office, a huge smile on my face.

It was nearly lunchtime, and I was hungry. Since I was nearby, I put myself on Sid's clock and went down the road to check out Joe's Bakeshop and Drive-In.

Joe's is located on Michigan Avenue, only a mile east of Hughes Investigations. Built like a fifties drive-in, the place features curbside service as a gimmick during the summer time.

I wanted to see the inside, though, so I parked the car near the road and hoofed it into the ordering area.

The place was nearly identical to Nouveau Deli. The cases were along one wall, with the cash register at one end of them. One other case, filled with doughnuts, croissants, and muffins, lined the right side wall. In the back was the kitchen area and the grill, where they made all the sandwiches. They had two tables inside, which, of course, were filled at this time, since it was lunch.

Joe's was not as busy as Nouveau Deli can be during lunch, but it was busy enough to be annoying. I spent the time while I was in line scoping out the place. Two women took orders, and then rang the orders up. It took a long time the way they did it.

At Sid's place, two persons took orders, and there were two cashiers, one for takeout orders, one for eat in. More efficient.

In the back of the restaurant, two guys made sandwiches with agonizing slowness. I grabbed a napkin, hid it behind my clutch purse, and noted their descriptions, as well as those of the two order takers. I also looked into the kitchen, but couldn't see anyone in there.

Finally, after an interminably long time, I placed my order for a turkey, lettuce, cranberry sauce sandwich and a Diet Coke. To go. I paid for it, then waited and watched some more.

The more I looked at it, the more the deli looked dirty to me, though in no way I could put my finger on. Of course, Nouveau Deli was known for extreme cleanliness, so it might just be a touch less clean and it would look much worse.

I checked the tiles, and noticed the same pattern as Nouveau Deli's, a blue and white random bathroom tile. There were pieces of corned beef on the floor, but that shouldn't be too much of a surprise in a deli. I spotted a cockroach, but didn't say anything. For all I knew, they'd gotten their cockroaches from the bread bakeries in Oak Park.

I doubted, even though they said they were a bakeshop, that they baked their own bread.

Besides the four persons I'd already written a description of, I saw no one else in the deli who might be construed as working there. Was Joe a real person, and if so, was he anywhere on the premises?

What exactly was I trying to find? I realized now that I had a lot to learn about investigating.

Just looking around, I could see more than a few health code violations. There were no thermometers to be seen, either in their refrigerator cases or their warming heaters. They were supposed to be there by law.

A chicken salad of some type sat on the counter, unrefrigerated. God knew how long it had been there. Three hours or more, and it's worthless; should be thrown out. The bleach bucket I spotted under the coffee machine was cloudy, to the point of being charcoal gray. My guess was it should have been changed about two hours ago. Certainly, I wouldn't have wanted to eat at a table that had been wiped with that solution.

After thirty minutes, the sandwich maker called my name, and handed me a bag with my order in it. His apron was filthy, smeared with stains of mustard, catsup, and bits of brisket. He probably used his apron as a knife wiping implement. One thing for sure, Joe's was not the place to talk about Nouveau Deli's sanitation procedures.

In the forty five minutes I'd spent at Joe's, I didn't see anyone I recognized. But then, the problems had started after I left, so if there was a double agent, I might never have even met him or her.

At home, Peyton still banged away at the panelling upstairs. "I'm back," I yelled to be heard over his hammer. The hammer stopped, and I could hear his footsteps coming down the stairs. "What's that I smell?" he asked as he opened the door.

"A sandwich from Joe's," I said, and pulled it out. "God knows, Peyton, I don't know how they stay in business. This thing might kill us."

"Oh, I doubt it, d'Arcy," he said. He grabbed one half of the sandwich and stuffed it into his mouth. "After all, you are a bit biased," he said, his mouth full. He took another bite. "Tastes okay. By the way, there's a message from Jennifer on the machine. I talked to her, and when she started rattling off your schedule, I told her to call back and leave it on the box."

"Boy, Sid wasted no time telling them I was back, did he?" I swallowed a bite of the sandwich. The turkey was strangely warm. I personally liked my turkey cold when I ate it in a sandwich. It signaled to me that it was refrigerated until I got it. I walked toward the phone, which sat in a little niche made especially for it in the living room.

"By the way, some guy named Tim called."

I spun around. Had Tim cancelled on me? "What? What did he say?"

Peyton laughed. "Honey, I read you like a book. He wanted to move the meeting time up to 5:30. Said that would give you guys more time for dinner before you went to the show. Might want to call him and confirm. I left his office number on the phone table." He went into the kitchen to pull out some Diet Pepsi for both of us.

I walked over to the phone nook, and dialed Tim's number first. He was out, but I left a message with the secretary that 5:30 would be fine. Then I pressed the answering machine button. Jennifer's high girlish voice spoke back at me. "Hi, d'Arcy, I'm so glad you're back. I'm giving you some supervisor shifts, since I've been averaging five a week, and so has everyone else.

"Let's see. Monday, supervisor 6-3; Tuesday 6:30-3:30, cash; Wednesday 6:30 to 2. Thursday you have off, Friday's 6-3. Saturday I have you 11-9, cash first half, floor second half. Sunday you have off, since I know you always liked that. I know it's a lot of hours your first week back, but we've been real short-staffed. Love ya, honey."

My heart sank as I wrote my schedule down. Forty six hours on the line did not give me much time to do any investigation off line. I'd have to mention to Sid that this kind of schedule wouldn't work.

It was 2:30. I sat down with my sandwich and watched a low-fat cooking program. After that, I went upstairs and helped Peyton with the panelling tear down. I told him I'd accepted a job at the private investigator's place, and he said he'd have to take me out to celebrate on Saturday. "No dice, guy, Saturday's an 11 to 9 shift," I told him.

At 4:00 I called it quits, and ran down the steps to get dressed for my date. When I opened the door to my bedroom,

I found Pantera sleeping on clothes that Peyton had laid out for me to wear tonight. "Peyton, you sweet-hearted man, you," I yelled upstairs. I could hear his laughter from above.

Peyton had chosen a pink satin shell, to wear under a black satin suit. It was an outfit I'd forgotten I owned. Black patent heels were there, as were a garter belt and a pair of sheer black hose which had seams up the back. A note he'd scrawled lay under Pantera. I found it when I moved her off the skirt. "I'll do your hair," was all it said.

Peyton had been a hairstylist before he decided his true interest lay in interior design. He was as fabulous with hair as he was with Good Will furnishings.

Many of my friends, when they heard about Peyton, thought he was gay. He wasn't, although he'd never found the girl of his dreams. I've met many of his flavors of the week, all very beautiful tall black women. I don't know what he's look-ing for, but none of them have filled his expectations. That was fine with me. Fact was, he was a great housemate and some time workout partner.

I felt a little sluggish, and realized it was because I didn't work out today. I have a three on, one off workout schedule, and it actually was my day off. But I always feel a trifle guilty when I didn't work out. I shook off the feeling and went to take a shower.

I put on sultry makeup, gray smoky eyeshadow, deep red lips, pink blush high on my Russian cheekbones. I knew that was what Peyton would want me to do. Then I called him. He blow-dried my hair expertly so that the curls looked like Julia Roberts in *Pretty Woman*, and then he pulled up the back into an intricate do that was part Gibson, part Topsy Tail.

He added an antique brooch, circa Art Nouveau period, all onyx and silver in waves. "Stunning," he finally pronounced. I stood up and he patted my butt as I scooted into my bedroom to dress.

The doorbell rang as I adjusted my garter belt. I could hear Peyton open the front door. There was silence as Tim presumably stared at him. The muffled, "I was looking for d'Arcy Carter," floated toward me as I picked up my pace. I pulled on the stockings and straightened the seams. Oh, Peyton.

"Yes, this is her house," Peyton said, with a flair for the dramatic. There was a beat, at which point I figured my chances with Tim were finished. I stepped into my skirt and heels at the same time, then grabbed my jacket. As I opened the bedroom door, he said, "Don't worry, I'm just fixing her house."

"Don't listen to him, Tim. He is my housemate, but we're just friends. You spoke with him earlier, I believe."

"Yes, I believe I did." Tim shook hands. He looked marvelous, tall and blond in a black tuxedo and red cummerbund. He took my arm and led me to the car. I waved my thanks to Peyton, and we were off.

CHAPTER 6
"Out on the Town"

Tim's candy red Probe waited at the edge of my lawn. "Ah, the American car," I said. "Very nice."

Tim smiled as he opened the door for me. "You like?"

"Mmm, it's okay." I ducked into the beige seat, careful to sit first before I put my feet inside. This particular skirt was extremely narrow. I'd have ripped it otherwise.

"Nice legs," he said. He shut the door and went to his side of the car while I attempted to hide my blush. "But then, you're a bodybuilder, I shouldn't expect less."

I laughed. "So, to the Whitney, right?"

"Right." Tim turned the car around and headed toward Middle Belt Road. Construction on I-94 had closed the Middle Belt Road interchange, so I suggested he use Michigan Avenue.

He nodded. He drove from Dearborn into the city. The neighborhoods went from clean, to less clean after about a mile. Slightly further on, the shops had barred windows, the houses had plywood boards in the gaping window holes.

"Hey, I took your advice," I said. "I just got a job with a P.I. firm."

"You did? Great. Which one?"

"Hughes Investigations, on Michigan Avenue in Inkster."

"You mean Ralph? Good people. Good people."

"You know him?"

Tim nodded.

We hadn't said anything for several minutes. I tried to think of a way to broach the subject of what he knew about Nouveau Deli. He found Woodward Avenue and turned north. The three story Victorian house turned restaurant rose to the left shortly thereafter. "Ralph's done work for the firm on occasion," Tim said, breaking the silence. "You may end up working for us sometime. You ever eaten here before?"

I shook my head. "Speaking of restaurants, I'm going back to Nouveau Deli."

"What?" He looked at me in surprise and nearly drove past the valet, who tapped on his window. "Oh, sorry," Tim said, as he looked back around and opened the window. "Do we just leave it here?"

The young man nodded. His tuxedo matched Tim's, except that he wore a fuchsia cummerbund. My door opened. Another young man took my arm to help me out.

I hesitated, then turned in the seat and stood up. I felt like I'd performed the second half of a sissy squat. It didn't feel particularly ladylike, but I wasn't sure what I'd done wrong. If you start dating a lawyer, d'Arcy, you'd better take a refresher charm class.

You'd never know it to look at me or my manners, but the fact was, I came from a rich Grosse Pointe auto family. Three generations. Add this to the mix: my mother descended from Russian royalty, and escaped between the wars. I was the black sheep in the family. I got the recessive upstart gene. I've never known how to act in polite upper crust company.

I met Tim on the other side of the car, and we walked up

the steps and past the bird fountain to the front door.

Indoors, the entire house looked like it had been bathed in pink plaster. The maitre d' ushered us into a room at the front of the house. The ceiling had elaborate circular molding along its edge, and a dazzling crystal chandelier hung in the center. The tables had white linens and pink napkins folded like rose blossoms, placed in the water goblets. Peyton would have approved.

The waiter pulled the chair out for me, at a table next to a window. Lace curtains puddled on the floor below me. The house felt almost too cool. The smell of cream sauces hung in the manmade breeze.

"Would Monsieur care to look at the wine list?" The sommelier appeared at my elbow while I got settled. Tim nodded and looked at me for confirmation. I agreed, and opened the menu.

Having been a bodybuilder for seven years, I was somewhat at a loss in the French-style restaurant. It's not that I disliked cream-based sauces, but after so many years on a low fat diet, I found it hard to digest them.

But I would have felt uncomfortable ordering a chicken breast poached in white wine, so I tried to find the healthiest meal available.

I finally decided on the least expensive chicken dish, since I knew Tim was a new lawyer with lots of student loans still outstanding.

The sommelier came back with the wine list, and Tim turned his attention to that. Tim pointed to it as he shared it with me. Together we picked a California Sauvignon Blanc by Quivira, bottled about three years ago. We gave our orders to the waiter, and then sat back.

"Now what's this about you and the deli?"

I explained about Sid's visit and the impending case work. When I finished, Tim asked, "Well, did Hughes back you and say it's part of his investigation?"

I nodded.

"Good. Then you are officially launched as a private investigator in training."

"So it seems. I hope I can do a good enough job at this."

"Oh, you will." I watched Tim's face as two sides of him battled about something. Then he said, "Look, this goes against confidentiality, but I know I can trust you to be discreet, and I think you should know about this."

"Is it a lawsuit?"

"Yes."

"Food poisoning?"

"No."

That surprised me. "Why is Nouveau Deli being sued?"

"Look, I can't tell you the details. And I'm sorry for that. Suffice it to say the place is falling apart. Breaking apart is more like it."

Whetting my appetite and then taking away the meal. "Oh, Tim, can't you just—" But then I stopped myself. No, d'Arcy. Prove to him just how strong you can be. If you do your job right, you'll figure it out on your own.

I turned to look out the window and compose my thoughts. Time to think of something else to talk about. But all I could think of was how much he looked like Jeremy, the last man I'd ever loved, the time we went to House Parties weekend our senior year at Princeton. Just before we'd broken up.

Tim rested back in his chair. I could feel his eyes on my cheek. He gazed at me for a long time. Almost too long. I turned my face back to his.

What was he thinking? Why had he asked me out? It's not like d'Arcy W. Carter to attract a man like Tim, a man who was busily establishing himself as a corporate lawyer.

The sommelier came back and showed the bottle to Tim and me. I looked down at my plate. Tim tasted the wine, then indicated that the sommelier should pour. He did so, then left the bottle in an ice bucket in the corner of the room.

Tim lifted his glass. I followed his lead. "To your beauty, d'Arcy."

I blushed. "Well, thank you," I said. I could think of nothing better to say. My mother always said I was bad at accepting compliments. I hesitate to say everything else she's told me I was bad at. We clinked glasses and I took a sip. "Kind of sweet, isn't it?" I said.

"Well, I would have said it has a dry finish."

"Oh."

"Fruity, though."

I swirled my glass, watching the wine raise and lower along the side. I put the glass down, and Tim reached for my hand. He held it, and I looked at him. His eyes were so serious, I nearly flinched. They bored into mine, unrelenting, as though he were searching. For what? Did he want me to say he interested me? What was I supposed to do?

"I'm sorry," he said. "I'm not usually so forward. It's just, I've found this month, I can't stop thinking about you. The guys at the firm have been laughing, asking what in hell happened up north to make me so scatterbrained."

I laughed, somewhat stupidly, I thought.

The salads came, and, as suddenly as it came up, he dropped the subject. I supposed I should have been relieved. After all, I'd thought about him, too. Instead, his confession made me want to go back home and never see him again. The last relationship I'd had ended three years ago. It had been an unfulfilling relationship, one of many since the end of college.

After graduation, Jeremy dropped me and floated off to tackle Nepal. Three days before, he'd asked me to marry him. I'd never gotten over it, never could figure out why he really left. Worse yet, Tim's eyes and his feathery hair reminded me so much of him, my heart hurt.

The waiter brought the dessert cart up, but Tim waved it away. "No, thank you. Coffee and a check please. We're trying to make the show." The waiter nodded, in a way that made me think I'd heard his shoes click. I expected a "Heil" to issue from his lips. We drank our coffee quickly, then left the restaurant.

Princeton and my parents tried to instill a sense of culture in my life, but opera never stuck. My musical taste has always leaned more toward Malcolm McLaren's post modern form of Madame Butterfly. But we could have sat through worse stuff than "The Student Prince." It was lighthearted, the actors laying heavily on every pun. If I were to judge Tim's reaction, we stood on the same ground. He clapped, laughed at the jokes, but didn't seem moved by the music.

We left the box seats he'd gotten. I felt guilty that we'd had such good seats. They should have been saved for someone who truly enjoyed opera. "How'd you get these seats?" I asked, to make conversation as we waited for the stairs to clear.

"My boss couldn't go tonight. He's got season tickets."

"Ah, to be a lawyer," I said.

I watched the people below me. One woman, hair tied in a chignon, stood below me. She wore a black velvet gown with a keyhole cut out of the back. Her boyfriend or husband stroked the exposed small of her back. They kissed. I felt a tremor in my gut as I realized Tim watched them, too.

All the beautiful people, in tuxes and long dresses, shades of pale green, peach, and black. All of them seemed more beautiful than yours truly. What could Tim see in me?

After dessert and dancing, Tim took me back to my house. We were silent most of the trip. The air in the small car smelled of sweat and cigarettes. When he pulled up to my house, Tim turned off the engine. We sat and listened to the car's undercarriage clicking into coolness. "I had a great time," Tim said.

"Me, too." Was he going to kiss me? I felt like a kid. First dates send people back to being sixteen years old. I'd spent more than forty eight hours with him little more than a month ago, and we'd talked for hours without watching the time. Call it a date, and we were both tongue-tied. I opened my car door. He opened his and hurried over to help me out of the seat. He pulled me up. Before I got my balance on my heels, he kissed me. We hit our noses.

"Stop laughing," he said. We tried again, and again hesitated so we could match noses. After a moment of terror, I relaxed into it. I wanted it to last forever.

I got another attack of self-doubt as I took off the last of my makeup. Did Tim like me or not? Didn't every date say he had a good time, whether he had or not? It seemed too good to be true. Hell, it probably was.

CHAPTER 7
"Light on the Case"

The day after Independence Day, I went back into captivity—it was my first day back at Nouveau Deli.

Monday morning at five o'clock, the alarm rang. I groaned and got out of bed, then smashed the clock into submission. No one should be forced to see this side of the morning. The sun had barely raised its bleary head over the horizon.

I dragged myself into the bathroom.

Within a half hour, I'd dressed and eaten some oatmeal, and I was ready to go. I grabbed my bike helmet and headed out the door.

It was a ten mile trip to the deli, through a section of town that wasn't the greatest. Up Middle Belt Road, hang a right on Michigan Avenue, and go through a rough area of Inkster. Luckily, at 5:30 a.m., no one was awake, and I've never had trouble. Besides, I can ride pretty fast on my bicycle when I have to. I knew from experience it took me about a half hour to ride to the deli.

I realized halfway there that my stomach had tied itself in knots. My heart beat hard in my chest, so hard I couldn't hear myself think. This job had always made me feel inadequate, and today was no exception.

I made it in twenty five minutes, and locked my bike at 5:55 near the dumpsters behind the back door. I knocked on the door until one of the bakers finally heard me and opened it.

"Hi, Brian," I said to the man who let me in. Brian'd been at the deli for three years. He was a middle-aged man, very taciturn, but he knew how to make coffee cake. He didn't answer me, but went straight back to work.

I punched a new card in the clock, then entered the main order area to begin prep. The deli had two large refrigerator cases and one small one. One case held salads, while the other held all the desserts. The little one had a few deli meats and cheeses. I didn't have to fix up that one. The night workers cleaned and rearranged it after close.

I pulled the plexiglass off the front of the salad case and went to work. First I pulled off all the plastic wrap which kept the salads clean overnight.

Usually, when I arranged my salads, I put dark or colorful salads next to paler, mayonnaise based salads, so the case would look pretty and appealing. Today, there was a propensity of white. I ran to the kitchen to see what else they planned to bring out during the course of the day, then went back to my case.

I had twenty four salads in there already, and five more would come out in the next three hours or so. Since the case held only twenty four pans on the bottom comfortably, that meant five salads had to go on top, where they were not refrigerated. No mayo mixtures, no cheese or meat based salads could go up there, or they'd go bad in three hours.

My pickings for the top row were slim. I finally chose a few vegetable vinaigrette salads to go there.

Then I arranged the rest of my salads along the bottom of the case, and labelled each one in the space between the plexiglass window and the reefer unit. Finally, I lined the case with an assortment of pop cans. This trick sold drinks and had the added benefit of keeping the metal pans from moving when we dished out the salads later on.

I put the plexiglass back on just as Cecille Brown came in the back door. She punched in while I opened up the dessert case, then walked along the side of the store to her post at the cashier stand.

Cille had worked at Nouveau Deli almost since the day the deli first opened. She was the first person hired after Sid, Lynnette, Kelly and Charlie realized they'd need more people. After all, they didn't want to work eighty hours a week. She was a short woman, very athletic, like me, although she preferred softball, tennis and golf. She had short, curly blond hair and a no-nonsense approach to the work we did. Why she never became a manager, I never knew. She'd probably have been a good one.

I've always been a bit intimidated when working with her, because she knew her position almost too well. She was quick to point out what I had or hadn't gotten done. My heart did a little backflip as I watched her open her cash register and start to count change. I hadn't wanted her to be here the first day back, when I was bound to mess up something.

Actually, Cille and I got along just fine during our off time. We'd gone out for coffee or the movies together, and we had other interests in common as well. She just made me nervous when we worked together.

"So you're back," she said. She counted the pennies in her drawer while she spoke. "We've been real short-staffed since you've been gone. Three others quit our line after you left. We're glad you're here."

"Yeah, Jennifer seemed elated when she gave me my schedule. She gave me forty six hours this week."

I looked at my schedule report to see who else would be here with us. I saw Jennifer's name, and breathed a sigh of relief. To Cille's determined speed, Jennifer was relatively unflappable and unhurried. They drove each other crazy, but I liked working with Jen. "Speaking of her, where is she?"

Cille's face twisted strangely, but then the look left her, and she said, "Management, in all their wisdom, has been cutting hours. She'll be here at 6:45 instead. Oh, and did you notice they also cut out your second order taker that used to come in at 10:30? 'Obviously, we don't need that extra person Monday through Thursday,' they said. Shows what our managers know. All they care about is profit."

"Making decisions without watching the line again, huh?" That was an unwelcome piece of information. I'd have trouble getting everything ready before we opened. "I'd better get my act together then."

I turned my attention to the dessert case, and Cille and I worked in silence for a few minutes. Why had they been cutting hours? It was probably one of Charlie's bright ideas. Nouveau Deli was notorious for trying to make as much money as possible. But it was stupid to cut workers' hours in the summertime, when the deli was at its busiest.

It pointed up the fact that Sid had to be really scared to hire a private eye for twenty five dollars an hour.

Once she was finished counting her drawer, Cille put the muffins and coffee cake on serving plates and arranged them along the top shelf of my case, while I arranged the refrigerated desserts.

"Hey, d'Arcy, I bought some great yarn a few days ago. You'll have to come by and see it. Ribbon yarn, for a summer sweater."

As she said this, I recalled some of our after-work bitch sessions. We always did these at her house, always while knitting. Along with being an excellent supervisor, Cille was an unstoppable gossip off the line. I might be able to get some much needed background information at one of these, if I were tricky.

"Hey, I've got a project I've been meaning to start," I lied. "Want to get together some time this week, shoot the shit?"

"I'd love it. Make it Wednesday, all right?"

I agreed. After I labelled every dessert, I put the plexiglass in, and settled down to preparing the salad bar and soup set up.

Jennifer walked in, her blond ponytail swinging back and forth behind her. She waved hello to me, and started counting her cash drawer. She locked it back up when she was done.

At seven on the nose, Charlie Foster, the day manager, walked in, late as usual. He should have been here before I got here, but then, managers can get away with murder. He didn't bother to check in with me, but instead unlocked each door, and headed back to the office.

"Asshole," Jennifer muttered.

"D'Arcy, you forgot to put spoons in the salads," Cille said.

As I'd expected, Cille had figured out what I'd left undone. I started to walk back there to rectify my mistake, but Jen said, "I'll do it, d'Arcy."

"Thanks. Then, when you're done, could you run to the freezer and get me two cheesecakes?"

"You're going to need four today," Cille said. She grabbed a handful of serving spoons and put them into the offerings in the dessert case, since that case was closer to her than to Jennifer.

I looked over at my dessert case. There were four whole cheesecakes sitting there. I'd thrown out five pieces today because they'd gone moldy. And it was Monday, our slowest day of the week. "Jennifer," I said, and put up two fingers. She nodded and left.

The cheesecakes reminded me that I hadn't done my quality check. Only I could be hired to find out who was doing the food poisoning and then forget to test my own salads. I hurried over and pulled about thirty forks out of the white dishwasher drains which held them, and tasted each salad with a clean fork.

Unfortunately, two expensive salads, the Chicken Oriental, and the Hot and Spicy Shrimp, had gone bad. The chicken tasted sour and the shrimp tingled in my mouth from the fermentation. Much as I hated to do so, I weighed the salads out and threw them away. Nearly one hundred dollars down the drain, but it was better than selling them to a customer and then having them complain. Or sue. Or die.

At eight thirty, I told Cille to put her lunch order in.

She nodded, and looked in the case. "Oh, nothing appeals this early in the morning. What I really want is a nice, juicy ham sandwich. I think I have to have a ham and swiss grill today."

"Cille, you always have a ham and swiss grill," Jennifer said.

"Not always, but I gotta admit, I love the ham we use here."

"It's good, but it's not that good. It's just Virginia ham."

Cille ignored Jennifer, and wrote something on an order pad, and put her order on a clothes clip which hung along a wire. The order ticket moved slowly by electricity toward the sandwich maker's station, where the sandwich maker read it, and made the sandwich by the time the order packager saw it. Eventually the clothespin would wind its way back to us and we'd use it again. It took the contraption exactly fifteen minutes to make its rounds.

I double checked everything while we waited for her order to come up. I had everything labelled. Jennifer brought some salads from the kitchen, nearly slipping on the slick floor near the salad case.

"You okay?" I said.

"Yeah. Damn floor." She added the new salads to the case, I checked to make sure refrigerated things were under 42 degrees and thus out of the danger zone. Our heater case foods would come out at 10:30, just before lunch began in earnest. As far as I could tell, we were ready.

Cille left on her lunch break and I watched the register. Ten minutes later, I told Jen to put in her order. She stepped around to the front of the case. "I don't know what I want. Maybe rice pudding?" She gazed into the case for a moment. "Hey, d'Arcy, the light looks funny. Could you check it?"

"Funny what way?" I swung the sliding window to the right, a little hard. As I did so, the flourescent tube fell from its housing under the top shelf.

I shrieked, threw my hand into the case and grabbed the tube just before it shattered into tiny pieces on the cheese cakes and dessert pans. If it had broken, it would have sprinkled into the apple sauce, rice pudding, fruit salad and cheese cakes.

CHAPTER 8
"Death by Potato Salad"

"Jennifer, help!"

I needn't have said it. Jennifer had already run to my side. She reached in from the other window to steady the tube. I guided it through my window, and we laid it on the counter. I called maintenance, who said they'd be in soon.

When I hung up the phone, Jennifer said, "Good catch." We both laughed helplessly, relieved that we had averted the near disaster. "How 'bout that break order?" I asked when we finally calmed down enough to breathe, and she nodded.

"I'm not real hungry, for some reason," she said, and started laughing again. "Oh, d'Arcy, thank God you moved as quickly as you did."

Shortly after the fiasco with the flourescent light, Cille came back. She noticed the tube on the counter near her register. "What happened?"

I explained the incident to her as Jennifer brushed past us, break in hand.

"Geez, that could have been a good mess," Cille said.

"Good wasn't exactly the word I was thinking."

The maintenance man came in. A new guy, I hadn't met him yet. He set about re-attaching the flourescent tube. "Hi, I don't think I've met you," I said.

He looked at me over his right shoulder. "Michael Nader. I don't think I've ever seen you here before."

"I was away from the job for a month or so. When'd you start here?"

"Two weeks ago."

I wanted to ask him where he'd worked before he came to Nouveau Deli, but I couldn't think of a good way to do that without tipping my hand. I would read his application after I got off the line today.

"Did this look as though it were hanging strangely before it dropped?" he asked.

"I'm not really sure. Jennifer asked me to check the case, and when I slid the door back, it went." I tried to remember if it had been hanging incorrectly when I set the case up earlier. Nothing had seemed wrong. "Maybe one of us knocked it out of its seat when we were setting up."

"Hmm," he said, but he seemed unconvinced. "Just seems strange is all. Tombstone wasn't right."

"Tombstone?"

"The thing it hangs from." That was all he said to me. Soon after, he left, and I continued to wonder what he'd meant by the fact that the tombstone wasn't right.

I took my break. When I got back, Cille said, "Jen and I took some time while you were gone to rearrange the salad case, I hope you don't mind. Give us more room."

I looked at their handywork. I was not surprised they'd redone my salad case. I had a practical style, not a pretty one. But I had to admit the case looked better after they'd done it.

Organized to the point of being anal, Cille had found room for every salad, including Mom's potato salad, which I'd had to pull out. Jennifer had then stepped in and made the case beautiful, with Hershey bars as garnish.

By 10:00, the deli was ready for the lunch rush. It began five minutes later, with three phone calls in quick succession. Cille picked up the first, always the quickest one to act.

Jennifer manned her station as take-out cashier, and picked up the second phone as it rang. The third was mine. I was afraid to pick it up and leave myself with no order takers at the counter. I knew from experience, though, that no one else in the deli would bother.

I'd been right to worry. By the time I turned around, three customers had gathered. I took one order, Jennifer pitched in for the second, the phone rang again.

I felt the flutter in my chest I hadn't felt since I'd quit. Five more customers came. Jennifer was helping a pick-up customer. I nearly ploughed into Charlie. He was dishing out some potato salad. I went for an order pad. Now why couldn't he pick up an order pad and help for just a minute? But no. Asshole.

At 11:30, the line was out the door. Phones rang constantly. When I noticed Cille was ringing up people at the same time she took orders on the phone, I realized I had to get away from my line to find someone to help me.

I checked with the sandwich makers, but they needed one more person, also. Muller, the sandwich maker supe said, "If you call anyone, tell 'em I need someone, too. We're running twenty five minutes per order. Where's management when you need 'em's what I say."

Twenty minutes was our maximum time allowance per order. They must have slowed down the "clothesline" that we hung the orders on, and I hadn't even noticed.

I called back to the office area. Why on earth had they cut back on people when we clearly needed five sandwich makers and at least four service people, even on a Monday?

I could hear the customers grumbling behind me, angry there was no one to take their order.

Charlie answered. "Charlie, I need an order taker; Muller needs a sandwich maker."

"So?"

Why should I have expected any other answer from him? I recalled a similar situation with Charlie when I screamed that I would quit over the phone at him. Before I could do it again today, I broke the connection.

Hadn't I seen Sid come through earlier in the day and head back to his office? I tried his extension, and luckily he was in. "Sid, I have a problem and I need your help. I need an order taker, Muller needs a sandwich maker, and that fuck head Charlie won't help me."

"Hey, great, some business. I'll be there in a second. But d'Arcy, please watch your mouth. I don't want customers hearing that kind of thing."

"Yeah, yeah." I went back to orders. In seconds, Charlie had joined the sandwich makers. Another few seconds, and Sid was at my side. He winked at me and picked up an order pad.

The next two hours went by quickly. At 1:30 I asked if Sid would stay on the line for five more minutes. Then I told Jen to change bleach buckets and wipe down the line between customers, and I went to the kitchen to get salads.

When I was on the line, I could tell I wouldn't be able to concentrate on my investigation. My remote control took over, and I found myself worrying more about supervising than about who was responsible for the food loss. Once I got off line, I pulled Sid to the side, and said, "Hey, I'm scheduled for forty six hours."

"Well, Jennifer thought you'd want as many hours as possible," he said.

I shook his biceps with my hand. "Do I have to spell it out for you? I thought I was supposed—"

"Oh," he said. His eyes widened. "Say no more. Lower hours coming at you." He pulled away from me, looked both ways, then left to go back to his office.

I wished I could get Sid to lower the hours right away, but that would seem suspicious, I supposed.

I checked out with Charlie. I refused to even talk to him. Instead, I took a sheet of paper, wrote down how many people we had and how many we were short, plus what we'd run out of during the course of my shift. I threw it his way when he left the sandwich makers' line, and then followed him back to the office area.

Working here for God knows how long would be a joy at this rate. I had quit the deli because of Charlie. There were more reasons, of course. What he'd done that day was just icing on a cake that had baked for a full year.

But all I could see when I looked at him was that Friday, phones ringing off the wall, a Ford representative breathing down my neck expecting me to make a mistake, my chest was screaming, in so much pain I thought it was a heart attack. I was understaffed and underpaid, and he'd refused to help me.

Argh!

He went to his cubicle. I stopped at the filing cabinet.

I willed myself to calm down and not think about that day. I had a job to do. I was not being paid twenty five big ones an hour to chew at a wound that should be healed by now.

I wanted to check the actual food loss tracking sheets for the past few weeks, to get a feel for when the marked upswing in loss had occurred. I thumbed through the filing cabinet until I found the "Food Loss—Daily" file.

The tracking sheets were neatly kept, most recent week on top. That was the one Sid had showed me the weekly rollup of. The week before it had even higher losses, totalling $2500.

No wonder he'd decided to do something about it. A quick calculation told me $2500 over the course of fifty two weeks was a loss of $130,000, just for one department. A deli couldn't live for long with that kind of loss.

The week before that had also been high, but the one from the beginning of June had only been about $1000. In May, all food losses combined totalled less than $1000.

So the shenanigans must have started almost exactly the week I quit. I wrote down a few notes, then pulled out the day by day sheets, to see which shifts had the highest losses. There were several each week, almost always in the afternoon, that totalled over $400 in a shift.

Who was the supervisor on each of these shifts? I thought the question had an obvious logic. Maybe that supervisor didn't do his or her job very well.

As a supervisor, it was my job to check each salad at the beginning of my shift, to make sure nothing went bad overnight or while the prior supervisor was busy. But that was just a security blanket.

I personally also knew exactly how long I could expect each salad to last. For example, a fresh vegetable salad in vinaigrette should really be sold within a day, because it would look limp and nasty the next morning. A potato salad or bean salad, on the other hand, could handle a few days of being in the case; some of those were actually better the second and third day.

A supervisor worth his or her salt would peg the salads that had to be sold that day, and push them. Pushing a salad was easy. After someone ordered a sandwich and drink, I'd just say, "And would you like a little Pinto bean salad with that? It's especially nice today." If that routine failed to work, I'd discount the salad a bit just to move it out.

A supervisor who was sloppy, on the other hand, or new to the job, might have missed the fact that the salmon pasta had been around for a couple days, and let the salad go without trying to boost its sales. Maybe this was what was happening.

I checked the top of the page, but there didn't seem to be a rhyme or reason to who'd supervised. Some of the days, Jennifer suped. She, of all people, would never intentionally miss a salad. She was an extremely organized person, which was why she'd been chosen by Charlie to do the work schedule every week.

She had, as I recalled, an almost uncanny ability to recall when each salad had appeared in the case. No, when she was on shift, the salads had not been left simply to rot.

The other supervisors who had high loss rates were Ted, Chan, and Doody. Were they all trying to send a message to Sid by sabotaging him? For some reason, I doubted the problem was that widely spread.

What if it wasn't the sandwich and salad line supervisors who were in on this? The other obvious choice was the kitchen. They were the only other department who handled salads on a consistent basis. Hell, they made them.

I pulled another file from the drawer, this one the list of kitchen supervisors for each day. I looked through the month in question: Brian, Ned, Ned, Lydia, Ned, etc. Well, less names to choose from, but a propensity of bad salad days had occurred when Ned was on shift. That was interesting, and bore looking into.

What else should I check while I was here?

New people. People who could also be plants from Joe's Cafe. I wondered how many people had been hired since I left. That question had a simple solution that I didn't feel like trying out. But I really had to.

I was about to get the nerve up to broach the question with Charlie, when I heard a sudden movement in his cubicle, like he'd scraped his chair hard when he stood up. Then Charlie rushed past me. He nearly knocked me down.

I was about to yell at him to watch where he was going when I noticed he'd headed into the bathroom. He slammed the door behind him. Was it my imagination, or had he looked white, almost green?

Ah, shit. Was he the next food poisoning victim? A strange satisfaction passed over me. Then I realized what an awful thought that was.

Oh, God. And it had happened on my shift.

"Charlie?" I called. I knocked on the door. I heard the

door lock snap shut. He'd locked me out. "Charlie, what's the matter? C'mon, man, what's up?"

I heard a wretching sound, long, deep, which gave way to dry heaves, another wretch, a gurgle. Then all was quiet. "Charlie?"

No answer.

CHAPTER 9
"Panic Sets In"

"Charlie?"

I couldn't hear anything. I tried the door, even though I knew he'd locked it.

For a second, I panicked. I couldn't think of anything to do. Oh, God. I could feel this investigation slipping out of my fingers.

"Sid?" I yelled. His office was right around the corner from the bathroom. He didn't answer right away, so I ran around and told him, "Sid, something's wrong with Charlie. He ran into the bathroom, threw up, and now I can't hear anything. He won't come out."

Sid's eyes got wider than I'd ever seen them. They fluttered a moment, and then he said, "Christ, don't let it happen again." He jumped up from his chair, ran around the corner, and pounded on the bathroom door. "Charlie, come on out. Charlie." Then, Sid started to bawl. "Oh, God, don't let this happen to me. Don't let this happen. Not Charlie. Oh, God."

I felt like I was floating up in the air, or that I was watching this on a movie screen and it wasn't really happening. But Sid was panicking even more than I had. I calmed myself as I watched him, then I pulled him away from the door.

"Sit down here," I said, grabbed a chair and pushed him into it. "I'll break the door down."

"What? You can't do that."

"Let me break down the door. We might be able to save him."

Sid nodded, still bawling. I closed the door to the office area, then set my shoulders perpendicular to the door, and ran into it. The door shuddered and creaked, but didn't fall. I set myself up again and rammed the door, and this time I splintered the top portion. Using physical force finally cleared my mind. I'd be all right.

One more time, and the door gave way. I fell into the bathroom.

The small space smelled of bile and vomit. Charlie had missed the toilet, and the vomit was on the walls and floor, a curious black-green in color. I almost threw up myself, just looking at it. Charlie was in the center of the bathroom floor. He lay in a pool of the stuff. He wasn't moving. I checked his pulse, yelled at the same time, "Sid, call 911."

I couldn't find his pulse, so I stood up and ran back out of the bathroom.

Sid hadn't moved. I picked up the phone, dialed, and spoke as soon as the operator answered. "Yes, we have a medical emergency at Nouveau Deli. Please send an ambulance, and have them come to the back door."

I gave her my name and the address of the deli. She assured me an ambulance was on its way. I hung up, and turned to Sid.

He sat and stared at me. "Oh, God," he said, "I'm ruined."

"Stop it, Sid, let's think this through."

Sid was being no help. I'd have to do the legwork myself. What should I do while I waited for the ambulance to get here?

I snapped my fingers and ran into Charlie's cubicle. As I had suspected, his plate still sat on the desk, dried leftovers from his lunch of nearly four hours ago still on it. New England ham and potato salad and chicken salad. Fortunately, I hadn't sold any today at lunch.

Wait. New England potato salad? Very odd. Very odd indeed.

The chicken salad was from the sandwich line. My guess was it wasn't the chicken salad that had made him sick. If the salad was bad, too many people would have noticed. But one could never be sure.

"Sid, did you sell any New England ham potato salad today?"

He just shook his head, bawling and moaning.

I left Sid, who still cried silently in his chair, and went into the restaurant. "Check your chicken salad," I said to Muller, who was still on the sandwich makers' line.

"There's nothing wrong with it."

"Just do what I say, Muller. Check it, make sure it's not bad."

I could feel his stare going into my back. He hated being ordered around by a woman. I headed for the salad case. I pulled out the New England ham potato salad, weighed it up and then dumped it. I didn't even bother to taste it. I could tell just smelling it that there was something wrong.

If Sid hadn't sold it, and I didn't, chances were no customers would get sick, thank God.

Funny thing was, I didn't remember seeing it in the case when I set up this morning, didn't remember it there when I performed my quality check, and didn't remember seeing it on the kitchen's list to be made today. In fact, I knew it hadn't been there, because I hated every ingredient in that one, and I hadn't wrinkled my nose at it today. But somehow it had appeared in the case prior to lunch.

Damn it. Somehow, I'd failed at my job.

I reached the office again just as the paramedics entered the back door. I could see curious onlookers behind them. They probably wondered why an ambulance had pulled up behind Nouveau Deli.

I showed the emergency team into the office, then the bathroom. I gripped Sid's shoulder as we watched them trying to revive Charlie. God, I'd hated the man, but I would never have wished him dead. I shivered.

"Oh, God," Sid said.

It wasn't five minutes before one of them said, "We're sorry, there's nothing we can do for him. We'll transfer him to the hospital, but it's going to be a DOA."

I nodded. I'd expected that. He was probably dead before I even got to him. I hadn't been able to find a pulse.

What was it about me, only a month pretending to be a private investigator, and this was my third homicide case? "I'll call the police," I said.

"No, no, don't do that," Sid said. The look in his eyes was one of terror. "You can't do that. You'll ruin me. Oh, God, Charlie, please, you can't die." He started to wail again. I almost started to cry just hearing it.

"I have to. Let's face it, Sid, it's a suspicious death. Try to hide it, and you'll be worse than ruined." I went to the phone and called 911 again. "I need to report a death, I think the police should come. The ambulance is already here."

I thought Sid would start crying again, but instead, when I got off the phone, he finally seemed calm. "I suppose we should call Karen."

Tears finally sprang to my eyes. I nodded. Karen was Charlie's wife. She also worked part-time at the deli, in the meat and cheese department. I don't know how she put up with Charlie, since he was really a prick. But they'd met at the deli many years ago, and they'd had what I'd call a tolerant marriage. She was bound to be upset by his death. "Do you want to do it?"

"Yeah, I'd better."

"Better call Lynnette, too," I said.

I saw the panic flare up in his eyes again as I mentioned his partner. I wasn't sure why. But then the look faded, and he nodded.

The police came. They wrote notes for their reports, took pictures from every angle of the bathroom, and talked to the paramedics. It was hard to tell if they thought it was wrongful death or just the result of someone choking on his vomit during a bout with the flu.

I told the police I could give them the plate he'd eaten from, and I went to get it from his desk. Mysteriously, it had disappeared. "I'm sorry," I said, "I thought I'd seen it here."

"Is there any more of the salad around?"

"Oh, God, I didn't think of that. I threw it out, because I didn't want anyone else to get sick." Great. Let them know you think it's food poisoning. Failure again. Was I really cut out for this job? "I should have saved it, shouldn't I?"

"Where'd you throw it out? We can just take the bag."

"Oh, that's a good idea. Hang on."

But it wasn't that simple. Someone had already tied up the bag, removed it, and replaced it with a fresh trash bag.

I ran back to the office and explained. "Do you want me to search the dumpsters till I find it?"

"Doesn't matter," Sergeant McCall said. "The autopsy will reveal if there were any toxins in his system."

After they left, I turned to Sid. I was probably just lashing out in frustration as I said, "What the hell do you think you're doing, destroying evidence?"

"What do you mean?" He shrugged his shoulders, as if to say he had no idea what I was talking about, but he lowered his eyes.

"You know damn well. Having that plate cleaned before the police could see it may have seemed like a great idea at the time, but the fact is, they'll figure out it was food poisoning from the autopsy. It's always better to level with them, you should know that."

"Who said it was food poisoning? Who said that? Maybe it wasn't."

"Sid, get yourself together. Have you ever thought of the fact that you or Lynnette might be next? Hindering the investigation is not going to help us solve this before another person is hurt, or killed."

Sid suddenly sat down. His shoulders caved in toward the center of his chest. His hand went to his face, as though his head had become too heavy to hold itself up. "I can't believe it. Charlie, he was one of my best friends. Since college."

I hugged him, rocking him back and forth, knowing I had no comfort to offer him.

He continued speaking after a moment. "Oh, d'Arcy, maybe it's too late. When the health department finds out, we'll be closed. I should just cut my losses."

"No, Sid." I sat down next to him and pulled his chin up so I could see his eyes. "Look, I didn't put that salad in the case this morning. It wasn't there for me to quality check. It was planted when I wasn't looking. You were right. Someone is trying to sabotage you. And now, someone's killed Charlie. I don't know how and I don't know when. But by God, I'll find out. I'm going to find out who it is."

Or I'd never be able to keep my job with Hughes Investigations.

CHAPTER 10
"A Big Mistake on my Part"

Now that my food poisoning investigation had become at least one murder investigation, I felt nearly unable to handle it. My first reaction was to see what Ralph Hughes could tell me to do.

Since his office was on my way home from the deli, I debated how to go about this. Finally, I decided to do my workout first. Working out usually cleared my head, so I can think rather than react. And I'd been reacting all day. Besides, Hughes' office was on the way home, while the gym was in the opposite direction.

I pedalled over to Powerhouse gym, and performed a back and chest workout. My heart wasn't really into it. I was more worried about the death of Charlie than I was about my pecs and lats.

After about forty five minutes, I knew I'd made the wrong decision. This workout wasn't clearing my mind. If anything, I was feeling more muddled than before. I finally cut the workout short.

I may have hated the man, but I never wished Charlie dead. Who had? Had it been planned that he should die, or was it an unexpected mistake on the part of the food poisoner turned murderer? Unpremeditated manslaughter: weapon, food toxin.

When I finished my workout, I was ashamed at myself for not having remembered it. Really, a bodybuilder should pay attention when working out. We needed to feel the muscles, so we could concentrate on them to make them grow.

But I had just a few other things on my mind.

I biked the six miles to Hughes Investigations, and broke a light sweat in the comfortable afternoon sun.

I knocked on the door when I found the door locked. But no one was there. The lobby was empty; all the lights were off. No one answered my knock.

Of course. It was already five thirty. Why hadn't I thought about that? I could have done my workout later, but I'd decided to be lazy about biking here and then back to the gym. I'd mistakenly thought the workout would do me good.

Idiot.

Instead, I'd missed a talk with someone who might be able to sort out what had just happened. D'Arcy Carter, investigator extraordinaire.

This had not been a good day so far.

I rode back home to silence. Peyton was nowhere to be seen. Pantera slept in the open window of the living room when I came in. She barely opened one eye to make sure I wasn't some stranger she'd have to investigate. Some attack cat she turned out to be.

Woe was I. No Peyton to talk to, nobody at Hughes Investigations to talk to. Maybe I could call Tim.

Bright idea, but for ten minutes I argued with myself before I could get myself to do it. My mother had been the kind of woman to insist that a real lady never asked men out. I may have been raised in feminist times, but I still heard her voice every time I even thought about calling any man.

Finally I got up the courage, and told myself he might be able to help me with my investigation. I called his home. No one there. I hung up, drummed my fingers on the back arch of the telephone receiver. It took another five minutes to convince myself to call Tim at the office.

A woman's voice answered. "Hello, you've reached the offices of FitzRandolph and Roy."

I waited a minute before I realized she wasn't an answering machine. "Uh, hello?"

"Yes?"

"Yes, is Timothy Reams in?"

"Hold on a moment, I'll check."

While I was on hold, I tried to will my heartbeat back to sixty beats a minute. It felt like it had doubled its speed. I was on hold a long time. Long enough to pour myself a glass of cranberry juice so I could have more carbohydrates in my system. Long enough to pray, please God, maybe I've missed him. Maybe he's on a date with some other gorgeous chick, and I can just forget about him.

"Mr. Reams here."

"Hi, Tim?" My heart flip-flopped into yet another uncomfortable position.

"D'Arcy. How you doing?"

"Oh, all right, I guess. I was wondering if maybe you were available this evening?"

"You sound depressed. Did you lose your job or something?"

"No, nothing like that." I had twirled the phone cord the whole length of my pinky. The fingertip was bright red with the blood that couldn't get out from its tourniquet. I untwisted it. "No, it's much, much worse. Food poisoning has turned into murder."

"Murder?"

"Why, Tim? Why does everything I do turn bad?"

"Ah, d'Arcy, it's not you. What I think you need is a drink some place."

"Yeah, maybe you're right."

"Look, I'm finishing something up here, I should be done in fifteen, twenty minutes. Want to meet at TGIF's or something?"

"How 'bout you pick me up?"

"Oh, yeah, sure, I forgot you don't have a car. I'll be there in thirty minutes." We both hung up. I dropped my head forward, stretching my legs and back as I tried to get my blood pressure back to normal. Here I go again, courting another romantic disaster.

It took me only fifteen minutes to dress in my good jeans and a red and white striped button down shirt. I put on some mascara, lipstick and blush and called myself finished. I considered eating something, but the doorbell rang before I could decide what.

I grabbed one of my jean jackets in case it got cold later, which was pretty doubtful. This July so far had been the hottest one I could remember. I put my wallet in my back pocket and left the house. When I reached his black BMW, I said, "Thanks for coming. I had no one to talk to."

"At your service," he said. He opened the passenger door for me. "Is TGIF's okay for you?"

I nodded. TGIF's was a chain restaurant situated on the outside of the circular drive around Fairlane Mall. It tended to be a bit loud and raucous, which was what I thought I might like tonight.

We were seated by a window which looked out toward the mall. The maitre d', a terrific looking black man who reminded me of Peyton, only smaller, handed us the menus.

"Let's have some fun," Tim said. "You order me a drink and I'll order you one. No telling until we get them."

"Okay." I looked through the menu. There were thousands of drinks with ridiculous names. Some of them I knew from my days in college, when I'd been well on my way toward an alcoholic future.

In those days, Princeton had rites of passage that were

mostly alcohol related. I remembered one time when a friend of mine and I went to a party, where there was a different theme drink in each room. She and I had two drinks in each; Pina Coladas, Daiquiris, Manhattans, Alabama Slammers.

All I could remember of that night was the faint smell of tropical paradise. I landed in the Infirmary that night with near alcohol poisoning.

Come to think of it, that had been the last time I'd gotten really drunk. I felt sick to my stomach for eight days. After that I turned to weightlifting and left drinking behind.

The waitress came up, breaking me out of my memories. "What would you like?"

Tim spoke first. "The lady will have an Alabama Slammer."

The waitress's left eyebrow raised up, and looked over at me. I nodded. "And he'll have a Snake in the Grass."

He laughed. The waitress left.

"No offense meant, of course," I added.

"So, when are you going to get a car?"

"God, I have to, soon. Since I came back from Grayling, I've told myself it's time to grow up and get myself a set of four wheels. Be on the look out for me. Cheap, European or Japanese, one I can do my own repairs on."

"You're not asking for much, are you? You gave me such a rough time about my Beamer, I thought you'd buy American."

I drank from my water glass, then traced patterns on the condensation. "That would be admitting defeat."

"Excuse me?"

Tim didn't know about my history with my parents, or the fact I'd attempted to erase their effect on my life. His left eyebrow formed a question mark, but I didn't want to explain the situation to him tonight. I said nothing.

"So, tell me more about what happened today," Tim prompted, I suppose to change the subject.

"Oh, first day of work, and my manager, Charlie, dies of

apparent food poisoning. It seems as though he got it from a salad he'd gotten out of my case. Trouble is, I didn't put it there. I mean, I didn't put the salad there. I didn't put the food poisoning in it, either."

"Jesus. Food poisoning, huh. What do you think, botulism?"

"Well, in some ways, that would make sense. Botulism is the only one I know that can consistently result in death."

"Yeah, that's what I thought."

"But, you see, Tim, botulism only grows anaerobically, so it occurs mostly in canned foods. Nouveau Deli only uses fresh products in its salads."

The waitress brought the drinks. I sipped from mine. It had the sticky sweet flavor I remembered from the sloe gin. I sniffed at it after I tasted it, but all I could smell was juniper berries. No coconut, so it didn't turn my stomach.

Tim's turned out to be a Manhattan-like drink, made from Irish whiskey and sweet vermouth. In the glass, the brown liquid looked potent.

I took another sip. "God, Tim, I bet the police are going to look up the supervisor for the shift and come around asking me questions."

"Good guess."

"Meanwhile, I feel like I've failed Sid, and he looked so in shock. I don't know, maybe I will be out of a job. I've never been much good at anything."

"C'mon, d'Arcy, that's not true. Look. This is getting you depressed. Pick out the next drink you'll order me."

For the next round of drinks, Tim ordered a Sloe Comfortable Screw for me. Not to take the bait of the obvious sexual entendres, I ordered Tim a Kamikaze. Tim also ordered some popcorn.

"Are you hungry?" he asked. "I ate at work before you called."

"I may be hungry later." The truth was, at this point in time, I didn't feel very hungry, although before Tim came to pick me up, I'd been ravenous.

"Well, back to food poisoning. What else is there besides botulism?" Tim asked.

"Oh, lots of kinds. Staph, Salmonella, chemical food poisoning."

"Staph, like you mean a Staph infection?"

"Well, yeah, but if Staph is in your food, you're not going to get a Staph infection. You'll just get mighty sick. It's caused from people infected with Stapholococcyl germs."

"Meaning?"

I bent the little stirrer in my drink back, so it wouldn't poke me in the eye. "Well, something like 75 percent of the population carry Staph germs naturally. On their hands, in their noses and ears. No problem, as long as these people keep their bodies and hands clean."

"Uh huh."

"But if they stick unclean fingers into food, they leave Staph behind, and then the germs would multiply in its happy new surroundings. Voila, poisoned food."

"Sounds charming." Tim patted my hand, and drained the rest of his drink.

"The lady will have a Strip and Go Naked," Tim said.

I giggled. "And he'll have a Stinger." The waitress walked away. "I need a bathroom."

I stood up, and made my way back to the restrooms. My brain felt a bit jumbled. I could tell I hadn't done serious drinking in a long time. Two drinks, and I felt tipsy. I went to the bathroom, then splashed cold water on my face.

I straightened up at the sink, dried off my face, and checked my eyes and nose for any tell-tale redness. There was none yet, for which I was grateful. Then I walked carefully back to the table, and coerced my body to walk in a straight line.

"You okay?" Tim asked as I sat down.

"Yeah, fine."

He grinned. "Well, cheers." He raised his glass, and I realized that the drinks we'd ordered were already here. I picked up mine, clinked my glass to his, and drank.

"God, this one's sweet. What's in it?"

"Have no idea."

"You mean you order drinks with no idea what they are?"

"Just picked them because of their names."

I thought a moment, something that had become increasingly hard to do. "You're a very naughty boy."

"You are unusually attractive, d'Arcy."

"Emphasis on the unusual, right?"

"Come on, why can't you take a compliment?"

"I don't know, why can't I? My mom always told me that. I don't know. I've always thought I have weird features." I took another swallow. "Large mouth, small eyes, and a Roman nose, all aquiline."

"I think you're beautiful."

I didn't say anything for a moment. When I did, I changed the subject. "You know, if I were sabotaging the deli, I wouldn't want to rely on Staph. It seems a haphazard way to poison food."

Tim blinked twice. "Okay, I see your point. So what's left?"

"Well, chemical poisoning would be easy. Just put a strong dose of bleach in the salad."

"Yuck. Wouldn't someone notice the salad tasted like a nasty swimming pool?"

I giggled again, then felt foolish. "What have they got to eat in this place? I'm getting a bit drunk."

"You're not the only one. I guess I should have something, too."

The waitress came up. "What do you have to eat?" Tim asked.

She pointed to our placemats, which had a small list of appetizer like things. "That brie looks good," I said. I pronounced my words carefully, but could feel myself slurring. It was the l's and s's that got me every time.

"Another round?" Tim asked.

"What the hell?"

We laughed. Then Tim said, "Salmonella?"

"Here? Oh, you mean. . . .well, yeah, that's my guess. What with all the food loss we're having. Protein rich salads, left out over three hours. They'd still taste about the same."

"Kind of an easy, less obvious way to poison foods."

"Yeah, but it wouldn't necessarily kill the hapless guy. It's rare that salmonella leads to death."

"Well, maybe it was meant to be a warning, not a murder," Tim said.

"Funny, that was just what I was thinking. But a warning about what? And to who? Why was this Ben Mitchell guy killed? Oh, Tim, I don't know where to start."

He stroked my fingertips. "Seems to me you're doing just fine."

When the waitress came back, she set the brie between us, then gave me a Between the Sheets. I'd ordered a Tootsie Roll for Tim. Together we devoured the brie.

"So, Tim, now that I got you drunk, why don't you tell me what the lawsuit's all about?"

God, I was getting ballsy.

"What lawsuit?"

"Oh, come on, you know, the one that concerns Nouveau Deli."

"Bad girl."

"Oh, come on, I won't tell anyone. Hell, I might not even remember."

Tim laughed raucously. "It's a divorce. Nasty one."

"Divorce? Who? Charlie and Karen?"

He shook his head. "Unh-unh. Sid and Lynnette." He pronounced her name carefully. "She was having an affair."

"An affair? With who? Whom?"

"Dunno. He's out of the picture, I hear, but they're still splitting up. Be back in a minute."

I waited for him as he went to the John, and marvelled at

the way my head was spinning. Four drinks could do this to me? How many drinks had we had? Now I couldn't remember.

Wasn't there something I'd meant to ask Tim?

He came back to the table out of the fog. He looked so good, like a blond knight riding back from the Crusades, looking for his damsel in distress. Oh, Ivanhoe. He took my hand and helped me up, and we walked out the door.

Outside, the air was cool on my face. We stumbled toward Tim's car. After a minute or two, he said, "Where the hell is it? Hell, I've had too much to drive."

"Don't look at me. I'm wasted."

"Maybe we should take a walk."

I nodded.

We walked toward the parking lot entrance. I stumbled again on a curb. Tim helped me up. "Whoa, there, baby. Here, lean on me."

We meandered through the grass. It seemed the more I walked, the drunker I got. I don't remember how, but suddenly we were in the trees. "Tell the ground to stop moving."

"Here, sit down here until your head clears."

I obeyed, sitting down abruptly, Indian style. Tim kneeled down next to me, and turned me to face him. He kissed me, a french kiss, long and deep.

"I can't breathe," I said.

"Sorry." He kissed me again. Again. I sank back.

"God, that feels good."

It felt as though my insides had drained out of me. Tim moved next to me, fumbled with the buttons on my shirt. "God, your breasts." He cupped one in each of his hands.

When I woke up, I could feel pine needles digging into my scalp. I had no idea how long I'd slept, all I knew was that I was still drunk.

It was hard to breathe, and I thought I had alcohol poisoning. Then I realized it was because Tim was on top of me, asleep, his chin nestled into my neck and shoulders.

Oh, God, what had I done? I pushed Tim to the side, and felt down the length of my front. My shirt was unbuttoned to the waist, but still tucked into my jeans. My jeans were still buttoned. Thank God.

For a moment I'd been afraid that we'd made love. I didn't want to have sex with Tim when I was too drunk to remember. It would be another Jeremy all over again.

"Tim, Tim, wake up," I said.

He groaned and sat back on his heels. "You okay?"

I looked him up and down. He was fully clothed, nothing unbuttoned. Suddenly, I wanted to cry. What was he thinking? What did he take me for? A tease? I'd ruined everything.

"I want to go home," I said, sure I was turning redder the longer he took to realize what had happened.

CHAPTER 11
"An Unexpected Day Off"

Tim and I remained silent on the way home. He drove carefully. I stared straight ahead, noting everything outside the window. The beginning of a fog wrapped the trees and buildings in hazy shadow, everything light to dark gray. Maybe that meant it would be cool tomorrow morning.

A terrible ending to what had seemed to be a good evening. He didn't even kiss me good night, just waited while I fumbled for my key and made my way up the walk. He drove off as soon as I managed to open the door.

Well, I'd probably never hear from him again. Relief mixed with a painful yearning in the pit of my stomach, and for a moment I thought I'd be sick. Peyton was right at the door as I opened it. "Did you have a good time?" he asked.

"In a manner of speaking. I drank too much."

"Oh, honey," he said. "Here, let me get you a glass of water, so you'll feel better in the morning. Then, sit down, I've got some news for you."

I obeyed him. I sat down and drank the whole glass of water he gave me. He handed me two aspirin, which I also took. Peyton doesn't drink much, but when he does, he always goes through this ritual. He has sworn more than once that it's saved him the agony of a hangover.

He sat down next to me at the dining room table, and reached for a sheet of paper at the other end. "Here, read this."

He handed me the paper, and I looked at it. Everything was a little blurry, but I could tell it was a set of numbers. "What's this?"

"I talked to a guy today about the rifle stocks. Well, a few of them. The ones I knew the names of and stuff. That's what the guy thinks they'd be worth. He looked them up in his Gun Digest 'Modern Gun Values' book."

I looked again at the paper. '#1—Winchester 1886 Carbine, rare—$3,000-$5000.' "Three thousand dollars? In my attic? No way."

"It gets better. Those really nice ones, the gorgeous wood grain and everything? $2500 a piece or more. If we have a Browning Midas grade, it could be worth $5500. Of course, he hasn't seen the actual collection, but he wants to, before he makes us an offer on the whole set."

"Peyton, that's, that's, uh," I couldn't add it up to save my life. It was much too good to be true, and I knew I was setting myself up for a fall.

"Over twenty grand."

"Twenty thousand dollars?"

"It could pay for the entire upstairs renovation."

"Hell, that could pay for the balance of what I owe on this house, almost." I rubbed my eyes. My head had begun to ache. "This is too much for me. I'm going to go to bed, wake up tomorrow, and it will unfortunately be a good dream that went away. Good night Peyton."

"Oh, d'Arcy?"

I didn't listen, just went into my room, closed the door and collapsed on the bed. Now I remembered why I never drank. It was fun for a short time, that feeling of floating through life, but I'd screwed up a budding relationship with Tim, and now I felt sick to boot.

I dozed a few minutes, I guess, and woke to realize the light was still on. Then I remembered I should set my alarm for work tomorrow, since I was supposed to be supervisor again. Five o'clock would come way too soon.

That done, I lay back on my bed. The room was spinning. A boyfriend once told me—God, it was Jeremy. I could see him in the room, he bent over me, rubbed my forehead. "Put your foot down on the floor, it'll stop the room from spinning." I obeyed. I slept.

I woke, bleary-eyed, and tried to figure out what was making that awful noise. Oh, the alarm. I reached for it to hit the snooze button and instead hit the sleep button, which turned on music at an extremely high decibel.

"Ah, Christ!" I tried to turn it off, and had no luck. No button would shut it off. I was going to wake up the whole world at five a.m. Or at least Peyton and Pantera. I wasn't sure which was worse. So I wrenched the plug out of the wall.

What a way to wake up. Despite Peyton's reassurances, the water and aspirin last night had not warded off a hangover. The pit of my stomach felt hungry and nauseous at the same time, and my head pounded.

I dragged myself out of bed and into the shower. I didn't even bother to reach for the robe. If Peyton was awake and saw me in my glory, to hell with him. I looked at myself in the bathroom mirror and realized I was still fully clothed anyway.

I showered and brushed my teeth, which helped me feel marginally better, and then slunk back to my room. There I pulled on some leggings and a t-shirt. That way, if I felt up to a workout this afternoon, I wouldn't have to change. Ha, slim chance of that.

Though I didn't feel like any food at all, I forced myself to eat a bowl of oatmeal, and I drank a cup of coffee. The coffee made my stomach queasier, but at least it woke me up.

The ride to the deli seemed longer than usual. I almost missed the restaurant, though, because when I arrived, no lights were on anywhere in the place. Silhouetted against the early morning light, the place looked more like an abandoned warehouse than a bustling delicatessen.

In fact, the building had once been a warehouse, full of various car parts for Ford Motor Company. But the warehouse had gone out of business ten or fifteen years ago with the advent of just-in-time delivery or its precursors, and it lay vacant for three years before Sid and his partner, Lynnette, moved in and turned it into a thriving business.

I looked at my watch. 5:45. In spite of my hangover, I'd gotten here in record time, but I still didn't think I'd have beaten the kitchen people in. They were usually there at four a.m., because they baked the croissants and coffee cakes we sold every morning. Croissants take three hours or more, from start to finish.

Before I parked my bike in the back, I went to the front door. There, on a sheet of 8x11 lined paper, was a handwritten note in Sid's careless scrawl. "Nouveau Deli will be closed, Tuesday, July 6th due to the sudden and unexpected death of one of our managers. We are sorry if this inconveniences you in any way. The management."

Inconvenienced, hell. Why hadn't they told me they were going to close the deli? Here I'd come all this way, on my bike, with a hangover no less. . .

But then I realized this was a perfect opportunity to look around with no one looking over my shoulder. That was, if I could get into the building. On an off chance, I tried all the doors, even though I knew they would all be locked. It didn't matter if they were or not, because I knew all the doors were wired to an alarm system, anyway.

In my walk around the building, I noticed that the bathroom window was opened a crack, so if I could reach it, I might be able to get in.

I ditched my bike behind the dumpsters, and walked to the side of the building where the bathroom window was. It was open from the top down, only about four inches. As I recalled, we used a bar on the bottom half of the window to keep it relatively break-in proof. I also knew that for some reason, Sid and Lynnette had decided not to have the window rigged up to the alarm system. I figured either Sid or Lynnette were habitual key losers.

If I could remove the bar, I'd be able to get into the building relatively easily.

I climbed onto the ledge and struggled to keep from falling off the balance beam width of concrete. Tricky, when I was also battling the screwed up electrolytes caused by last night. When I physically moved my feet, it took my brain awhile to mentally register the new placement.

Workly slowly, I first removed the screen. This maneuver was simpler than I'd expected it to be. The screen had pulled away from the frame, so I was able to get hold of the release mechanism and pull it off.

I reached into the window and rather handily pulled out the bar. Within a few minutes, I was inside. I left the screen by the toilet, along with the steel bar. I planned to leave the same way I came in so I didn't have to disturb the alarm system, but I didn't want to make it obvious from the outside that I'd entered this way. I'd have to warn Sid about how easy it was to come in.

The alarm didn't go off. My memory hadn't failed me.

I'd entered through the bathroom where Charlie'd met his unfortunate end. The leftover vomit smell, though somewhat dissipated, made me want to throw up, too. I quickly exited the room.

Now I was in the office where the majority of the managers hung out when they weren't working on the floor. Take that to mean most of the time. This room I could search almost any time without looking suspicious. The opportunity right now was that I could search the rest of the deli in peace and quiet.

First I checked the owners' office. This was a smaller office behind the managers' work area, near the back door. This office was where Lynnette and Sid did their job, whatever that was. As far as I'd been able to tell, Sid controlled the action on the sandwich production line, while Lynnette oversaw kitchen production.

Both Sid and Lynnette managed their business with a practiced air of nonchalance, although Sid was better at the attitude than Lynnette was. No matter what emergency came up, Sid usually acted with grace and ease.

I remembered a time when I dropped an entire cash drawer on the floor, pennies and quarters and dollar bills flying all over the place. Jennifer, as supervisor of the day, looked on, dumbfounded, wondering how we'd clean up the mess. Sid breezed through and directed all customers to the phone-in cash register, as though it were the most natural reaction in the world.

Lynnette, on the other hand, sometimes felt the need for frenzied activity. If the deli were, God forbid, slow one day, the workers would not be. We'd be cleaning the rafters with toothpicks if it meant there was something to do. But she, too, could be a stable rock in a storm.

That was why I was somewhat surprised by Sid's obvious panic yesterday at the sight of Charlie's death. I was also pleasantly surprised by my relative calm in the situation. I had, indeed, learned something while at Nouveau Deli.

Their office was filled to the brim with file cabinets, samples of products, and computer equipment. Two cluttered desks sat in the center of the room, butted up against each other. From experience, I knew that Lynnette's faced the window, while Sid could see anyone who came in through the office door.

I looked through some of the papers on Lynnette's desk, careful to set them down exactly where I'd found them. There were buyers' reports, recipes for various coffee cakes, and other obviously food-related business, which included a run-down on produce prices for this week that she must have been comparing to last week's, since they were side by side.

I moved on to Sid's desk. In comparison to Lynnette's desk, Sid's was an absolute mess. Sandwich combination recipes scattered the surface, as well as a note from the payroll secretary which said checks awaited his signature. A lot of piles of paper, all filled with information I could make no sense of. There was also a file labelled 'FP' on his desk. Food poisoning? I opened it, but there was nothing inside.

Not a single thing on his desk directly related to my investigation, which seemed odd to me. I could understand that Sid would keep my investigation secret, but as far as I could tell, he seemed to be hiding the investigation even from Lynnette. Why? Wouldn't his partner be equally interested in the attempt to quell the food poisoning? But then, Sid had come to my house alone. Maybe he was still the only owner aware of the situation.

I went out into the hallway, then entered the kitchen. Everything was extremely clean. The stainless steel counters and dishwashers' area gleamed. Even the oven was devoid of grease. The room smelled slightly of the disinfectant bleaches and iodines.

I searched the room without really knowing what I looked for. I looked in the oven. Nothing. I looked under the three dishwasher sinks and the big automatic dishwasher. Still nothing, not even a leftover dirty pan. The kitchen looked even cleaner than usual, so I had to wonder if the deli expected a visit from the health department today. A good guess would be, probably.

I opened the freezer. First I checked the thermometer automatically. It registered ten degrees. Everything was carefully stored, the frozen pastries on top, meat on the bottom so any stray juice would not drip onto anything else if there was an unexpected thaw. Just as it should be.

I didn't spend long in the freezer, although I paused to press my burning head against the cold metal by the door. I closed the freezer door firmly, then moved on to the walk-in fridge. It, too, had nothing amiss. The thermo measured thirty six degrees. Perfect fridge weather.

Next, I checked the produce area. All the vegetables and fruits that didn't need refrigeration were stored neatly on wooden crates that had been turned on their sides to form shelves. The perfume of over-ripe bananas hung in the air, but nothing else looked in any way out of shape.

Suddenly, I realized my stomach was queasy again. I grabbed a small handful of grapes to suck on, hoping they'd help me out. I promised myself I'd throw some extra money in the cash stand my next shift to make up for my stealing ways. Honest to a fault, that's me.

From there, I checked the sandwich and salad area. This was my domain. With a practiced eye, I couldn't find anything out of place. I suppose since they probably knew by nightfall that they would be closed today, the kitchen had not made salads. There weren't many in the case, and those that were there they hadn't refilled.

The nearly empty silver pans in the nearly empty refrigerator case looked woebegone and depressed. I'd never really seen the case less than filled to brimming with a bounty of salads and desserts. But try as I might, I hadn't found anything yet that helped me in my investigation.

Was that a click I heard from the refrigerator going into defrost mode or from something else? Slowly, without a sound, I dropped to my knees behind the salad case. That was when I heard voices.

Because I'd kind of broken in, I didn't care to be found here, not by anyone. Tim once told me no matter what the mystery novels imply, breaking and entering wasn't tolerated, even by private investigators with good intentions. I had to get out of here without being seen.

I listened for a moment, and realized the voices belonged to Sid and Lynnette. They'd come in the back way, and had obviously just turned the alarm system off. I ran in a ducked position over to the door nearest me. No luck. Locked by deadbolt, only openable by key.

So my only avenue of escape was through the bathroom window, dangerously close to where Sid and Lynnette were. What was I going to do?

I snuck over to the sandwich production area, trying to inch my way toward the managers' office without being seen. It was then that I realized Sid and Lynnette seemed to be in the middle of an argument. That stopped me. I don't think I'd ever heard them fight before. What were they angry about?

"God damn it, Sid, what did you think would happen?" Lynnette said. "It's time to let go."

"No, if you want to let go, that's fine by me. Just sell your half to me, not to him. I mean, for God's sake."

I moved from the grill to the sink area, then hugged the white tile wall with my back. Quickly, I risked a peek around the corner into the hallway, in time to see them head into their office.

Lynnette's voice rose a few decibels. "Why do you want to keep on with a losing proposition?"

"It's my life—"

"Your life, my ass. Seven years is not your life. Besides, it was my life, too. If you'd really loved me—"

I dashed around the corner, nearly throwing myself into the managers' office. The bathroom was just in reach, but then I realized I couldn't close the door behind me. After all, I'd broken the thing into splinters when I tried to rescue Charlie yesterday. I hid in the corner behind the toilet as I figured out how to leave. The smell of vomit was stronger here. I nearly gagged.

"Oh, let's not bring that up again. Why did you agree to sell without even asking me?"

"And now with Charlie's death, how are we ever going to recover? The deli will never make it through this, Sid."

The door slammed, and then the managers' office door opened. I'd heard enough, and I was about to be caught. Time to high-tail it out of here.

CHAPTER 12
"Other People's Help"

Much as I wanted to leave without looking back, I had to be careful not to make it obvious where I'd entered. For one thing, I didn't want anyone to know I'd done a bit of breaking and entering. That wasn't something an apprenticed investigator would be applauded for. For another thing, I didn't want someone with less angelic reasons to follow my lead.

I had to make sure no one could watch me. I peeked around the toilet, and I could see no one through the door into the office. Could I make it out without being heard?

Just then, I watched Lynnette bustle back out of the managers' office. She slammed the door behind her. Then she and Sid started yelling at each other again.

Here was my chance. Much as I wanted to hear more of their conversation, I had to leave. I went through the window again, then carefully lowered myself to the ground. I reached in for the screen and steel pole. After I arranged the pole and window back into its original configuration, I had the screen reattached within a few minutes. Time to run to my bike.

I was at the street corner before I slowed down. Now what did I plan to do? It was only nine thirty in the morning. I hadn't expected any time off this week after I saw my schedule.

My first thought drifted to Tim. That thought was painful. He would be at work. And he probably never wanted to see me again. How could I have been so stupid as to get drunk on my second date with him? I'd ruined my chances with him. In the recesses of my mind, an old and forgotten memory came back to me, unbidden and unwanted.

I tried to push it back down before it crystallized. I concentrated on pushing my bike along the pavement, driving with no swerves of the front tire. Jeremy. Jeremy had seen me that night I'd gotten so drunk that I ended up in the infirmary. He'd taken me there, as I recall. But he'd never forgiven me for that. Forever after, he would refer to me as a lush.

Even though I'd never gotten drunk again. Until last night. Oh, Tim, what an idiot I was. And here was a man even my parents would have approved of.

I didn't realize I'd stopped riding. I stood, straddled on my bike, at the corner by the deli. A blue Escort passed me. For some reason, I caught sight of the woman who drove the car.

I knew her. I'd seen her somewhere before, and I knew the memory was far from pleasant. But why? Where had I last seen her? She was with someone, a large man I didn't recognize, so he didn't help me to place her.

I thought for a minute more, but it didn't come to me. My brain was still too spongy from the day before to have any memory at all. I swear to God, I will never drink again.

Maybe a gym workout would help. Weights had been my ticket out from what I thought would be sure alcoholism. Replacing one addiction with another. It could have been worse. Bodybuilding was a healthy addiction, and I'd kept it up to the point that now, after seven years, I could compete if I wanted to. Which I didn't, not really.

Today was my day for a legs and shoulders workout. That would be a good way out of my doldrums, I told myself. Squats are exhausting and at the same time invigorating. I decided to go over to the Powerhouse and do a light workout.

It took me ten minutes to ride over to the gym. Since I'd dressed for a workout, I went in and immediately started my stretches. Oh, God, my whole body ached.

I did squats, leg presses, leg extensions and leg curls, then went on and performed three sets apiece of four shoulder exercises.

In the middle of a set of front lats, I remembered who the woman in the car was. The local health inspector. One time, when I'd been working the cash register during Jenny's break, the woman came in and announced she was there to do the yearly health inspection.

I'd run around trying to find the manager of the day to escort her on her tour, all the time thanking God that even so early in the morning, I'd already placed my thermometers in all the cases, and the bleach bucket had just recently been changed.

So, I'd passed the health inspector's rigorous search.

I rested my head against the incline bench for a moment while resting between sets. I could smell the curious mixture of Endust-like disinfectant and old sweat that I figured was typical gym smell. It didn't do too much to settle my stomach, but the workout was making me feel better.

It didn't take a brain surgeon to surmise where the health department lady had been going when I saw her on the corner. Nouveau Deli. It also didn't take me long to decide that the reason we'd all had the day off was not to mourn the dead. The health department had had a hand in it.

A woman smiled at me from across the room. "You must really work out a lot, huh?" she asked.

I nodded, not really listening to her.

"Do you think you could show me your workout sometime?"

Inwardly, I sighed. Normally, I wouldn't have minded guiding her through a few of my paces right there, but my heart and my mind were on too many other things. I smiled weakly and said, "Sure, sometime. Not today, I'm afraid."

"Oh, no, I wasn't asking you to do it today. Just—"

"Look, tell you what. Harry, the guy behind the desk today? Leave your name and number with him, and I'll get back to you to set up a time."

She looked so encouraged, I felt kind of guilty. "Oh, that would be great. I really want legs like yours," she said.

"Thanks."

I headed out of the weight room wondering when I'd next be working at the deli. Would the place be closed down before I had a chance to finish the investigation?

The workout helped clear my brain a little bit. The electrolyte imbalance was less pronounced, so I could tell where my limbs were heading, but the headache and muscle aches were still present. Maybe it was my imagination, but I thought my pores reeked with the smell of a mixture of liquors. God, I hated sloe gin. Borrowing a towel from the front desk, I took a long, cool shower. Then I'd go have a nice salad some place.

When I was done, I left the gym and headed over toward Hughes Investigations, stopping for a bite to eat at a burger joint on the way. The red meat would do me good, I told myself as I talked myself out of the salad. It would reestablish my electrolyte balance. Uh huh, sure.

I reached the office at about one thirty. Genevieve was knitting again as I walked in. "Hi Genevieve. Afternoon coffee break?"

She laughed, I thought maybe with some guilt, as she finished the row. "Well, lunch, but I went a bit long. My daughter just went to the hospital with heavy contractions. I think she'll have the baby early and I won't have this done in time."

"I've had that happen. Can I look at it?"

Genevieve held out the piece she was working on. It was an aran pattern, a style of fisherman's sweater that had subtle patterns rather than the bobbles and fancy heavy cables seen on Irish fisherman's sweaters. "It's working into a lovely sweater, isn't it?"

"Oh, thank you, dear, but it's taking so much longer than I hoped. I still have the panties and booties to do, and I'm losing hope I'll get it done in time."

"Oh, it's okay if it's a little late, isn't it? After all, it's a gift from Grandma."

"You're such a doll, d'Arcy." She tucked the sweater back into her drawer, then turned to face me again. "What can I do for you? Here to see Ralph?"

I nodded.

"He's back in the office, but wait a minute." She pulled another drawer open and pulled out some paperwork. There was a contract, a W-4 form, and some other stuff she wanted me to sign.

"Can I claim a deduction for my cat?" I asked as I filled out the tax form.

She laughed. "I don't think so, dear."

"Oh well, too bad. Great. I guess I'm official now," I said.

"Welcome to the team. Maybe we should do a knitting night together."

"I'd like that." I waved as I opened the door to the back office space. Her mention of a knitting night reminded me of the night I'd set up with Cille. Was it Wednesday night? That sounded right. I couldn't forget that.

I could hear Genevieve as she announced over the intercom that I was there.

Ralph stood by his desk. I shook hands with him, and he motioned to the nearest chair.

"Are you okay? You look kind of tired," he said.

I didn't want to tell him how stupid I'd been last night, so instead I said, "Oh, I stayed up too late last night."

He grinned, his mustache pulling up as though he knew what I'd been doing. "So, how's it going?"

"Well, not so well, actually. My case has definitely turned into a murder investigation."

Ralph screwed up his face as though he'd tasted something bad. "Why didn't you let me know?"

"I came by the office, but you weren't here. It was about five thirty."

"Oh, damn. I should have thought of that. Make sure you get our home phone before you leave today. It's unlisted." He sat forward in his chair, elbows poised on the desk. "How'd it happen?"

"My manager ate some potato salad on my shift, and four hours later, he was dead."

"Was it a popular salad?"

"Excuse me?"

"Did a lot of people eat this salad, or was it one that might have sat around awhile?"

"Hmm. Not real popular, I guess. But the weird thing is, I was supervisor. I set up the salad case, but I didn't put that salad in there."

"So someone put it in when no one was looking. That's what you're saying."

I nodded, squeezing my lips together with my fingers. Did I see anyone add a salad to the case? Jennifer. She'd put in some salads during my break. I'd have to talk to her. "Can I have a piece of paper?"

Ralph handed me a pen and a notepad. "You must have thought of something."

"It might help. I don't think Jennifer is in on this. I've known her a year, and I don't believe she would try to kill someone, but I guess I can't rule it out."

"Have you found out anything else?"

"Oh, it might have happened during my break as well. Better ask her all she knows." I wrote my questions, then put numbers in front of them. I traced my numbers once or twice so they looked like bold-face. "Oh, sorry. What did you say?"

"Have you found out anything else?"

"I spent some time in the deli today. No one else was around."

"Closed after the murder."

I nodded. "It was pretty easy to get in."

"You're telling me you broke in." He sat back in his chair. I tried to read the blank expression on his face.

I lowered my eyes. "I'm not telling you anything. I'm telling you I used the managers' alternative entrance."

Ralph laughed. "You're smart. Just keep that to a minimum, please. B and E is not a good habit to get into as a licensed private investigator."

"Understood. I work there, found an unlocked door and walked in before I realized the deli was closed. The alarm wasn't even on."

"Right."

"Anyway. I looked around a bit, didn't see anything important. Checked everything. All legit, in fact, extremely clean. But one thing. At one point, the owners came in. I overheard them talking."

He raised an eyebrow.

"While I was in the bathroom. Let's just say, all is not peaches and cream with them. Sounds like one wants to sell the deli, the other doesn't. I want to follow that up." I made a note, and traced my number three.

"Tread lightly on that one. But that also bears looking into. Sounds like you're doing all right."

"Hmm. Then there's Joe's Cafe. How do I learn more about him and his operation?"

Ralph thought awhile, chewing on the end of a pen. "What is it you want to know about them?"

"What their interest is in Nouveau Deli. Would they try to make the deli look bad? I don't know. I guess I just want to talk to them. Well, Sid wants me to talk to them, too, I think."

Ralph dropped the pen onto his desk blotter. He raised his eyebrows a little. "Well, as your boss at the *Detroit News,*

I could ask you to interview him for a possible feature story. Journalists can learn some amazing things."

"That might work. Thanks."

Ralph opened one of his desk drawers and pulled out a white laminated card. He handed it to me with a wink. It was a press pass. I tucked it into my wallet.

"Have you found out any information on Ben Mitchell?" I asked.

"A bit. He lived in Dearborn, near Fairlane Mall. Owned a small house. His driving record was clean. His tax records list his occupation as government employee. I'm not sure where. I'm trying to track that down."

I whistled. "That's amazing. How'd you find that out so fast?"

He laughed. "Soon, d'Arcy. You'll learn the tricks soon. Keep in touch. Let me know what's going on, and don't be afraid to ask questions. That's what an apprenticeship is for, after all."

"Yeah, I will." I stood up, preparing to leave.

Then he said, "It seems to me, you're forgetting one obvious suspect."

"Oh?" I turned around to face him again. "Who's that?"

"Was Charlie married? Did he have a girlfriend?"

I stood up straight. "You don't mean I should suspect Karen of this, do you? She wasn't even in the deli yesterday."

Ralph shrugged. "All I'm saying is you shouldn't completely discount it before looking into it. 75 percent of all homicide cases, the spouse or lover did it."

I nodded, tracing a glass mark on the desk with my finger. "Yeah, I see your point."

"Good." He stood up. "You'll learn as you go along. You seem to have some natural talent, though. It'll be easy to teach you. By the way, Genevieve will be making up business cards for you."

"Thanks." I raised my hand in a wave and left.

CHAPTER 13
"Suspect #1—Me"

Since Jennifer's apartment was close to where I lived, I went there first before I pedalled home. I wasn't sure if she'd be there, but I decided to try anyway.

Jennifer lived in a set of red brick apartments, right off Michigan Avenue. It was a rough section of town, near where three policemen were shot trying to evict a black family that had taken up residence in a hotel but refused to pay the rent.

She lived with a big burly truck driver named Bronco, though, so I guess she felt safe enough with him around.

It had been awhile since I'd been to her apartment. I'd come last year, to watch Red Wings hockey on T.V. and eat turkey chili. As I recalled, her entryway was the closest one to the swimming pool.

I locked my bike next to the door I thought was hers and tried to enter. As I'd expected, it was locked; a secured entryway system. I'd sure want one of those in this neighborhood. I scanned the list of names until I found Bronco Benetti's, and pressed their buzzer.

Bronco's gruff voice came over the intercom. "Who is it?"

"D'Arcy Carter. Is Jennifer there?"

Without answering, he buzzed me in. I entered through the door, then tried to remember which apartment was theirs. I didn't have to worry. While I stood there, I heard a door open on the next floor. "Come on up."

I took the stairs two at a time so I wouldn't keep him waiting. Bronco is six four if he's an inch, has a thick black beard and wiry black hair, arms thick as construction barrels, and at least ten tattoos, mostly biker related. "Thanks, Bronco."

"Yeah, want anything to drink?"

"You got any ice water?"

He went into the kitchen and opened the refrigerator. He poured a glass and handed it to me.

"So, is Jennifer here?"

"She just got up. She's in the shower. Be out in a minute or so."

"She must've known the deli was closed today."

Bronco just nodded.

I sat on the couch, a green, yellow and once beige plaid that probably came from a parent or other relative. The apartment was spacious, with one bedroom in the back, near the bathroom. The television was tuned to a cooking show which featured creole food and a chef with a heavy southern drawl.

"Well, I wasn't told. Got there this morning to find it closed up tight."

Bronco didn't sit down. He stood, leaning against the wall which separated the kitchen from the rest of the apartment. He took a swig from his beer.

"How's the trucking business?" I asked.

"Pretty busy, now summer's here. I took a day off, though, today, when I heard Charlie'd died. Jennifer's taking it hard."

I was a bit surprised to hear that. "I thought she really didn't like him."

A female voice said, "No one liked him, d'Arcy, he was a

fucking jerk manager. Make enough money, you forget where you came from. But weren't you shocked when he hit it?" It was Jennifer, who'd just come out of the bathroom. I watched as Bronco's eyes turned to find her.

"I think we all were. I was in the office when he ran into the bathroom."

"Oh, God." Jennifer sat down on the purple bean bag chair with a thud. "Oh, God, that must have been awful. What do you think it was?"

It occurred to me as she said this that maybe not everyone was thinking it had been a food poisoning death. If someone's not involved in the investigation, and doesn't know there's been a problem, it wouldn't be the obvious first thought. In fact, maybe it hadn't been food poisoning, just a weird coincidence.

But I didn't really believe that. I was relatively sure the autopsy would find bad food in his stomach and intestines. Meanwhile, I'd better be careful, or I might mess up my cover. "Well, I don't know. I just know he'd been working on the production line just before he died."

Jennifer shrugged her shoulders, but I noticed a scrunched up look on her face. "If you could call it working."

"It seemed so weird," I said. "You know, dying of a flu. I guess it happens, but when you actually know someone."

"You think it was the flu?" she asked.

I shook my head to indicate that I didn't know what to think. "Man, can you die on salmonella? 'Cause my first reaction when I saw him run to the bathroom was, four hours after you eat."

"Food poisoning?"

"Yeah."

"But, d'Arcy, you tasted all the salads, didn't you?"

"I tasted all the salads I put in the case. Two of them had gone bad, but I dumped them, wrote them on the food loss sheet. Which salads did you put in the case? Because those were the only ones I didn't taste."

"Only the ones Brian gave me."

"Which were?"

She leaned back in the bean bag chair, looking at Bronco as though he might be able to answer the question I'd asked. "God, I think I put in some more Mom's pot, the one you put in the pop case, and some Chicken Oriental salad. Oh, and Szechuan noodles. They shouldn't have been bad."

"But did you test any of them yourself?"

She smiled down at the floor. "I snitched some of the chicken."

She hadn't mentioned the ham potato salad that had been on Charlie's plate in the office. "No other salads, though, huh."

Her eyes narrowed. "Spit it out, d'Arcy."

I wasn't sure how much I should tell Jennifer, but I really didn't believe she was behind the food poisoning going on at the deli. "Did you see who put the ham potato salad in the case?"

"You mean, you didn't?"

"Try to think. Was it in the case when you put the other salads in?"

Jennifer pitched forward in the bean bag. "I can't—no, wait. It was in there. I remembered thinking it looked oilier than usual."

"I didn't put it there."

"Who did?"

"That's what I want to know."

The look on Jennifer's face changed slightly, to one of fear and surprise.

"What, Jennifer?"

"Oh, just--You think it was food poisoning that killed him?"

I nodded slightly. "I'm scared because it happened on my shift."

Jennifer stood up. "I wouldn't worry about it, d'Arcy. You won't get into trouble. The kitchen has a new manager. Maybe he screwed up somewhere."

She stood over me, making me feel as though it was time

for me to leave. I stood up, asking, "Who's the new kitchen manager?"

"Ned Beyers."

"Ned? But he only started three months ago."

"I know." Jennifer's mouth screwed itself into a frown, then she smoothed her face back into a blank expression. She opened the door, waiting there to usher me out. Somehow, I got the feeling I'd overstayed my welcome.

"See you tomorrow?" I asked.

She shook her head. "Thursday."

"Hey, do you know where Charlie lived? I wanted to give my condolences to Karen."

Without speaking, she wrote the address on a sheet of paper. I took it and left.

As I headed toward my bicycle, I pondered why Jennifer had suddenly become so cool to me. The change had occurred as soon as I mentioned the ham potato salad. I had the distinct feeling she wasn't playing it straight with me, but I had no idea why.

Did she think I had poisoned Charlie? After all, I hated Charlie enough to quit unexpectedly just a month ago. And here I show back up just in time for him to get offed.

Or did she know who had put the salad into the case? I'd asked her if she knew that. She might have been sure I did it, or maybe she was protecting someone. But who?

And the fact that Ned Beyers had gotten the plum kitchen management job was also interesting. How had that happened? Ned was a hard worker, who'd been at the deli only three months, but he was considered by Lynnette to be a rising star. He'd come from another restaurant, where he'd worked as sous-chef for three years. She'd been the one to insist that he be trained as a supervisor for the ordering line after only a month on the job.

But rising to manager in three months would take more than talent, experience, and hard work. I'd been at the deli long enough to know it wasn't what you knew but who you knew if you wanted to be a manager there. That was why I hadn't stood a chance. Up until now, no one had made it to manager before working at the deli at least three years. It was, in fact, an abbreviated old boys' network. Thus, I would have expected another, well-established supervisor to get the kitchen manager job. Like Jennifer herself, or Cille, or Brian.

So here was more information I'd have to follow up on. All had not been lost by consulting with Jennifer, in spite of the fact that now she seemed angry with me.

CHAPTER 14
"Journalists of the World Unite"

I hopped back on my bike and checked the address Jennifer had written down for me. Karen lived in a relatively nice section of Dearborn, a bit far away from here. I didn't relish the thought of the long trip, but I rode fast with my head down, and it took me about twenty minutes.

The house was on a busy street, but it was in good shape for a nice city house. I hesitated for a few minutes, not wanting to interrupt the new widow's grief. But I convinced myself that it was my job to make sure I checked out every lead. And Ralph was right, many murders were simply the result of lovers' quarrels.

I locked my bike on her porch and rang the doorbell. After a few minutes, Karen answered the door. "Hi, Karen, I wanted to see how you were doing."

She nodded without reaction, and opened the screen door

for me. "The undertaker was about to leave. Thank you for coming. I could use some company."

I followed her into her living room, feeling guilty.

The furnishings were monochromatic, but Karen and Charlie had used fabrics and textures Peyton and I could only dream about: leather couch and love seat, marble and glass coffee table, hand-knotted Oriental carpet, all in shades of black and gray.

A tall, balding man stood up as I walked in, and bowed to me. "I think most of the plans are ready, Karen. I'll call if there's anything else I need." He squeezed her upper arm and let himself out.

"Can I get you anything, d'Arcy? A soda, some cookies?"

"No, thank you. How are you doing?"

Karen sank into the nearest chair and stared at the Oriental rug. "I can't believe it, you know? He was alive just yesterday. Thirty five years old, d'Arcy, thirty five years."

I leaned against the loveseat. "You seem remarkably calm. I'd be screaming, I think."

She looked up at me, and I noticed the vacant gaze in her eyes for the first time. "I was hysterical yesterday. The doctor gave me Valium to calm me down."

"Oh, Karen, I'm so sorry," I said, and realized that I meant it. Just being with her, I knew I couldn't believe she killed him. But I had to follow through. "Do you know how he died?"

She nodded almost imperceptibly. "Stomach flu, food poisoning, they're not sure which. Does it really matter? He's dead, for God's sake."

I nodded and cleared my throat. "Look, uh, it does make a difference. If it was food poisoning, it might have been, how should I say this? Planned, in some way."

"What are you saying?" Her eyes widened, showing her fully dilated pupils. "That somebody might have deliberately poisoned Charlie? I can't believe that."

"I know, I understand. Tell me, where were you when

you found out?"

"At my mother's. I went to her place about 9:30. She lives in Lansing. I had lunch with her. Then, I called the deli to see how Charlie—" She broke off, tears spilling down her cheeks. "Oh, d'Arcy!"

I went over, patted her shoulder weakly. "It must have been terrible for you. Oh, God, Karen." Suddenly I realized I was crying myself.

She grabbed my hand and squeezed it hard. "Look, I realize you and Charlie had your differences, but I'd really appreciate it if you came to the funeral."

"Of course, Karen. When is it?"

"Thursday."

The doorbell rang, and I went to answer it. It was Charlie's mother. I took the next opportunity to excuse myself.

By the time I arrived back at my house, it was after three. All I wanted was to drink a big glass of water and settle down for a long winter's nap. My head was pounding so hard I could hear ringing in my ears.

But the nap was not to be. Peyton was hard at work upstairs, pounding on the beams or whatever he was doing. Why on earth had I thought my home would be a safe haven?

I grabbed a glass of water and sat down at the dinner table, cradling my head in my hands. I wanted to scream, but didn't dare.

Peyton was only doing his job, a job I'd approved two months ago. It was my fault I still had the vestiges of a hangover, not his. I shouldn't take it out on him just because he was working hard upstairs.

I drank the water without stopping and poured myself another glass. I drank that one, too. I'd have to go to the bathroom in fifteen minutes.

What else was I supposed to do today? Something Ralph had suggested. Goddam Tim and the date I'd had with him. What a mistake.

It came to me as I considered having one more glass of water. Three thirty. Dead time at nearly any deli. A perfect time to call Joe's Cafe.

The phone rang five times before anyone answered. "Yeah, Joe's," a male voice said.

"Is Joe there, please?"

"Yeah, hold."

The man put me on hold before I had a chance to protest, which I probably wouldn't have done. What a terrific phone manner. Oh, well. That pointed out why Sid and Lynnette insisted Nouveau Deli employees should always ask politely if it's all right before they put a customer on hold.

After more than a minute, another male voice came on the line. "Joe."

"No, my name's Dee," I said, quickly deciding to shorten my name. "I'm with the *Detroit Free Press*?"

"Hey, lady, are you ordering or what? I don't have all day."

"Actually, I wanted to set up an interview with you, you know, for an article?"

"Really, an article on Joe's Cafe?"

"Well, I wouldn't have called you if—"

"Thursday at eight a.m. That's my slowest day, slowest time. Otherwise I'm booked solid."

"Thank you so much. I look forward to finally meeting you after all I've heard about—"

He hung up on me. If I'd really been a journalist, that kind of treatment would have immediately biased me to do a negative article on Joe. As it was, it made me think I wouldn't trust his business practices too much, since he treated his customers like crap. What was he up to?

Like a stupid idiot, I rationalized that since I was at the phone, I'd look around for messages from Tim. There were none, although I did find a message written in Peyton's neat handwriting saying I needn't go in to work today. That must have been what he tried to tell me last night after I'd closed the door behind me and collapsed on the bed.

I checked the machine for messages. None. In the insidious way my brain has, I'd already memorized both Tim's work and home phone numbers. But no, I would not call him first. That would only make things worse.

CHAPTER 15
"Mourning in the Morning"

At six thirty the next day, Wednesday, I walked in the back door of the deli, to the sounds of hysterical weeping.

As I put my work card into the time clock, I turned around to figure out who was crying. I finally realized it was Cille, her head resting on Brian's shoulder. "Cille?" I said, coming forward into the main area of the deli.

She pulled away from Brian, and I saw her face for a second before she shoved her head into my shoulder. It was covered with patches of red and white, as though she'd been hit with the flu and chicken pox at the same time.

"Oh, my God, d'Arcy, Charlie's dead!"

"Yes, Cille, sshh," I said, rolling her head back and forth to calm her weeping. "It's okay."

As soon as the words came out of my mouth, I realized what a ridiculous and uncaring remark that was. Cille pulled away from me, her face contorted. I thought of a Picasso sculpture called 'Face of a Woman', which sat in front of the Princeton Art Museum. I had nicknamed it, 'Lady in a Car Wreck." On the actual sculpture, the eyes were uneven, as though they'd been scrunched up or rearranged, painfully.

"D'Arcy, I know you didn't like him, but this is awful. I've known him five years." Cille started to wail again. "Five and a half years!"

Cille must have left the deli before Charlie died on Monday. I knew by looking at the schedule she was not supposed to work yesterday. Somehow, she had not been called during the ruckus. Brian must have been the first to tell her the news.

After fifteen minutes of trying to calm her down, I finally asked, "Cille, do you want to go home? You're really taking this pretty hard."

"I'm supervisor."

"I know. But I can take over for you and call someone in to be cash. Why don't you take the day off?"

"I can't do that," she said, her voice coming out in gasps and sputters. "Nobody but me takes care of the hygiene properly."

I tried to deflect the implied insult as well as I could, but I could feel its sting. In spite of what I knew about the case, I couldn't shake the feeling of guilt I had because Charlie had died after eating something that had been in my salad case.

"Cille, you're no help to anyone this way. If you insist on staying, you have to buck up. It's six forty five already, and look at the case."

Cille had barely begun her supervisory responsibilities. The plexiglass from the salad case had been taken off the front, but only three salads had been unwrapped. Brian and I helped her unwrap the rest of the salads, not trying for artistic presentation, and then I set about counting the change in my drawer.

By seven, the first case and part of the second were finished, and I'd counted the cash. Together, Cille and I worked on the second case and I started work on the baked goods.

Cille had withdrawn into herself to overcome her grief over Charlie. She didn't speak to me at all, but instead did her work like an automaton. I wanted to ask her whether she'd seen anyone put the ham potato salad in the case, but now did not seem to be the time.

By nine o'clock, I realized all our hurried preparation had been wasted. No one had come into the deli yet, even though we'd been open two hours. Could news of food poisoning have spread so fast? At least the Health Department had allowed the deli to remain open. My investigation wasn't finished before it had begun.

Cille hadn't seemed to notice the lack of customers, which was just as well. She refused to look at me. I felt sure she was blaming me for Charlie's death. Great. Now both Jennifer and Cille thought I was responsible.

Not that I could blame them. I'd suddenly reappeared after being away for a full month, and the day I come back, Charlie's dead. How much did the workers in the deli know about the fact that food poisoning had started to occur before I came back?

The day passed by so slowly I was afraid I was stuck in a nightmare. There were so few customers that Cille sent the phone-in cashier home as soon as he arrived, leaving just me and her to do orders and ringing up.

When I was done for the day, I passed Cille, who was checking out with Sid. "Are we still on for tonight, or would you rather not?"

At first, she didn't follow me. She must have forgotten our knitting plans. But then the confused look on her face cleared, and a look, almost of relief, appeared. "I could use the company, actually, if you're up to it. I might not be too talkative."

"That's okay. As long as it's all right for you."

"Seven o'clock? My place?" she said.

"Fine."

I really hadn't expected Cille to agree to the knitting night. Up till now, she'd acted as though the death were all my fault. Maybe she'd finally decided to trust me; she must have known I'd never try to kill someone.

After punching out, I headed to the office and opened the food loss files again. I knew the answer to the food poisoning problem resided in these papers, but I still didn't think I'd figured out the clue. I gazed over them with no further thought on my part, just trying to let the tao of the problem settle in on me.

According to the files I looked at, the food loss problem had intensified on June second.

That morning had routine losses, but that afternoon, Jennifer had to throw out fifty pounds of food. Inordinately high, especially compared with the week before that. The next day, Rodney lost twenty five pounds of food in the morning. Then a day went by with no food loss at all.

Tracking it, it seemed like five days of the week, there were large losses. The two remaining days usually had very few losses. What did that mean?

One thought tickled the edge of my brain, but didn't fully form. All I got out of it was the possibility that it meant one person was perpetrating this, and they worked five days a week. Yeah, that narrowed it down a whole lot.

I put the food loss file back into the filing cabinet, and went on to the kitchen file. Hector, the competent food manager we'd had for four and a half years, had left abruptly due to a heart condition. He'd put in his notice on May 15th, coincidentally the same day I left the deli.

Interviews, as far as I could tell, took place over the next two weeks. On June first, Ned had been selected as the new kitchen manager. At least, that was what I had to assume happened, since the file was scanty. But there was a letter dated June first from Sid and Lynnette, which welcomed Ned on board the management staff and asked all employees to congratulate him and cooperate to make the changeover a smooth one.

The start date of the food poisoning did seem to jive with Ned's job change, as Jennifer had suggested. I couldn't rule out just plain negligence and incompetence on his part as a reason behind the sudden problem. Ned had never worked in the kitchen, and could be unaware of kitchen policies and rules.

No, that couldn't be right. He'd worked as sous-chef for three years. Where?

I put the kitchen file back and went to the personnel files. From there, I pulled out Ned Beyers' employment file. Inside were his application, a training record, and his post training review. He had not worked at Nouveau Deli long enough to receive a six month review.

His application held clues as to why he'd been chosen for kitchen manager over any other candidates. He'd worked in food service for ten years, mainly in the Ann Arbor area. According to his job file, Ned had been a sous-chef at Bella Ciao right before coming to Nouveau Deli, for three years. Prior to that, he'd worked as short order cook at the Fleetwood Diner, bartender at the Bird of Paradise, and as manager trainee at a TGIF's.

A pang went through my heart as I recalled the other night at TGIF's. I pushed it back out of my mind.

So Ned Beyers certainly had experience to his credit. In fact, almost too much experience. Why had he taken a step down to come to Nouveau Deli and become a glorified counter attendant, probably for ridiculously low wages in comparison to what he'd gotten?

What was he making an hour? Where would I find out that information?

CHAPTER 16
"D'Arcy Carter, Hacker Extraordinaire"

Unless Ned had been chosen as the next manager, told he'd be the next manager when he came on board. If so, he'd been the first manager hired from outside the company rather than being promoted from the ranks.

But other possibilities also presented themselves with this information. A disgruntled kitchen employee could be the culprit. One who'd thought he or she should have been next in line for kitchen manager.

Brian, the long time dessert chef? Maybe Lydia, the talented woman who'd almost single-handedly invented most of the salad recipes? Or possibly another person, who had been passed over for promotion, was involved.

The more information I gathered, the more I stirred up the mud. I couldn't see a clear path anywhere. It was time to write down what I knew to see how far I'd gotten, before I forgot some of my leads.

For example, I needed to talk to Ned, but he wasn't in today. I checked his address and phone number in the file. I was surprised to find out he lived in Ann Arbor. Too far to ride my bike over there today.

Maybe I could call him. I used the office phone, called, and heard the message that the number had been disconnected.

Where would the office keep his newer number on file? My eyes wandered the empty office, and lit on the personal computer at the secretary's desk. Maybe they kept it in there.

Right now, a screen saver had been left on it. Fishes floated by in brilliant colors of red, blue, and purple. I touched a key, and the screen saver disappeared. A DOS prompt took its place. MS DOS? Why on earth did a deli making this much money have such an outdated operating system? How would I be able to navigate my way through DOS?

I wondered for a moment where Pam, the secretary, was, but I didn't want to waste any time.

I typed in 'DIR' and entered. A list of a hundred or so files scrolled off the screen. Great. How do I shorten the list so I can look at the files one at a time? Where was Peyton when I needed him? He'd recently taken a computer class at school, and he'd commented about the inordinate amount of time they'd spent studying this operating system.

Actually, if I could just remember the details, I'd taken a class on MS/DOS myself, almost ten years ago. I tried to remember some of the commands I'd learned for the then brand new IBM PC. Something with a slash, that's all I could remember.

I dinked around for awhile, worrying the whole time that Pam would walk in and wonder what the hell I was up to. Finally, I found a combination that seemed to work. When I entered it, the files came up in four neat columns. Some of it still ran off the screen, but I found two files I wanted to look at: ADD.WK1 and SCHED.WK1.

Fine. So how would I get into the files themselves? I needed to know what kind of programs they used.

I looked around. Still no Pam. How long would my luck keep going?

I glanced around the office, and since fate was still holding, discovered exactly what I was looking for. A LOTUS 1-2-3 manual sat right next to the computer. I thumbed through it until I figured out how to load a file, and then I was in business.

I pulled up addresses, and found Ned's new phone number. I jotted it down, plus the address, then exited the program. Now for the fun part.

I knew, from something Jennifer had once told me, that the salaries of all the employees were tucked into the back of the schedule file. I brought that file up next, and went to the end of the file.

And what I found amazed me.

I heard a noise outside, so quickly I scribbled down what I could, exited, and turned off the computer.

By the time Pam came around the corner, I sat with my head in one hand, the other covering the sheet of paper I'd copied it all on.

"Oh, d'Arcy, are you all right?"

"Yeah, fine, I just have a headache. Sorry, it's just that your chair looked so comfy."

"Oh, that's all right. I understand." She smiled at me as I stood up. I felt like an eel as I slithered out of the office. How long would it take her to realize the computer hadn't been off when she left the room? I didn't stick around to find out.

CHAPTER 17
"A Nasty Thought"

I went to do my workout before starting for home. While I did biceps curls, triceps extensions and calf raises, I tried to dredge up everything that happened over the last few days.

Right after the workout, I bought a pocket notebook at the drug store near the gym, straddled my bike and wrote down what seemed to me to be disparate pieces of information:

1) Sid hired me to find out who was producing the poisoned foods. Lynnette wasn't there.

2) Sid was blaming Joe at Joe's Cafe. Interview him Thursday.

3) A new kitchen manager started work the day before the food poisoning problem started.

4) Most of the poisoned salads are mayonnaise based.

5) Charlie was murdered. Was this intentional or accidental?

6) Maybe it's a disgruntled employee.

7) Jennifer is angry with me for some reason.

8) Cille is out of her mind over the death of Charlie.

9) Lynnette wants out of the deli biz.

10) Sid and Lynnette have been married for three years.

11) Before that, they lived together for six more.

12) Sid does not want to give up the deli. Problems in paradise?

13) Was it someone passed over for promotion?

14) Someone on the kitchen staff?

15) Was it Charlie's wife? I don't think so.

16) How did Ben Mitchell fit into all this?

I took out the folded slip of paper on which I'd managed to pilfer the salaries of a few people from the deli. Ned Beyers now made fifty grand a year. Next to this figure was a cryptic $16, which made me think that's what he made an hour before becoming manager. That was a hell of a lot more than my $6.25. No wonder he decided to work for Nouveau Deli.

I also jotted down a few other salaries that were interesting to me. There seemed to be no rhyme or reason for who got paid what. One thing was clear, however. Men across the board made more than women did:

Jennifer - $6.50
Cille - $8.00
Muller - $12.50
Lydia - $6.00
Hank - $11.75
Brian - $10.00

The best example was Hank, who'd started about the same time I did. He was making 11.75 to my 6.25 for the same work. And Cille, who'd been there since the day the place opened, made $8.00 an hour. No wonder so many people were pissed off at the management.

I made a mental note that I still needed to confront Sid about the possible marital strain between him and Lynnette. Why hadn't he let me know about this problem when he came to me? I'd just assumed they were hiring me together, and yet, it seemed as though she knew nothing about why I was back.

A sudden thought occurred to me, out of the blue. It had nothing to do with the case; it had to do with the rifles in my attic. Why had they been there? Why had they been covered over by panelling so that I didn't find them until forty years later? Were they stolen weapons?

A chill went through my body. The last thing I needed as a fledgeling investigator was to try to sell a bunch of stolen weapons.

I found a nearby pay phone and made a quick phone call. The lady at the police station told me she'd send a policeman over for more information about the rifles as soon as possible. I thanked her and hung up.

The skies had clouded over during my workout and phone conversation, and the air felt like a warm washcloth on my face and arms. The leaves had turned a curious mix of silver and dark green. I smelled ozone on the sidewalks and road pavement. Probably a thunderstorm was on its way. I huddled over my bike and pedalled home, moving slowly to keep from being overcome by the heat.

Had Tim called me today while I was out? Not bloody likely. What was I doing getting involved with him? I didn't stand a chance. This is what I considered as I drove down Michigan Avenue toward Middle Belt.

I've never had luck with men. There's no other way of putting it. Peyton and I got along great, but the reason was because we never considered dating each other. The moment we became more than friends, the easy companionship would be gone.

I'd already made that mistake with Tim. He'd reminded me too much of Jeremy, my long lost lover from college. Then, Tim began replacing Jeremy in my recurring sexual fantasies, and that was it. I could no longer hold a normal conversation with him.

It wasn't that Tim and I had nothing in common. In fact, I couldn't say whether we had similarities or not. I couldn't think of a single thing to say or to ask him when I was with him. I have stared at my plate more often than I'd like to admit when I've been in restaurants with him.

And that wasted get-together the other night. I didn't even want to think about that. Sure, the conversation had run smoothly when I was too drunk to think about it. When I was too drunk to remember what I'd asked him about and what his answers were. Oh, God, maybe I'd made it even worse. Had I embarrassed him with my questions? Had I embarrassed myself? He hadn't kissed me goodnight. What a telling sign that was.

I turned left, waving to some of the motorcycle gang members who lived a block and a half from my house. I've never spoken to any of them, but they've always waved at me when I go past, and have never done anything to scare me, so I guess we've lived in harmony for the last three years.

Then I turned right, left again on Paisley, and pulled into my driveway. Peyton's car was in the garage. I could see it through the open garage doors.

Peyton was in the dining room, writing something down on a piece of paper when I came in the front door. "Hi, Peyton, any messages?"

"Sorry, sugar, that good looking man who picked you up the other day didn't call."

"Don't remind me." I took the water container out of the fridge and poured myself a glass. "Want any oatmeal? I'm just making some."

"Girl, you and your oatmeal. No thanks, I'm trying to keep my figure neat and trim."

"Yeah, well, oatmeal does that for me."

"We have visitors coming in a few minutes. One's a policeman."

"Police? Why?" Already here to question the person in charge of salads just before Charlie's death?

"Well, I think you were the one who called him, weren't you? I got a phone call from the station, they said you'd requested one to look at the guns we found."

"Oh, that. Okay. He's coming already?"

"Now, why'd you go and call the police on this, man? Go screwing up the windfall before we can even try to get the money."

"That's exactly why. What if they're hot, Peyton?"

He laughed. "They've had forty years or more to cool their jets. Well, anyway, he's coming around the same time as the guy from the antiques shop who wants to buy the rifles we got. I guess they'll have to trace the weapons and see if they were stolen."

An odd wave of relief and fear swept over me. I was not looking forward to the questions I would have to answer on that inevitable visit when they realized I had been supervisor. "If they turn out to be stolen, will they try to blame us?"

"I don't think so, we just won't get any money. By agreeing to the police dude's visit, I guess we're considered innocent."

"Good. Yeah, that's fine."

I sat down to a big bowl of oatmeal with strawberry preserves and milk. I stirred it all together until the oatmeal turned light pink, but still had darker red and white swirls running through it. Peyton wrinkled his nose, but I ignored him. I was halfway through the bowl when the doorbell rang.

"I'll get it," Peyton said.

He opened the door. On the welcome mat was a small, stocky guy with thinning brown hair, and a slightly taller man with wavy gray hair and a heavy set of wrinkles. If it hadn't been for the uniform on the taller guy, I would have placed him as the antique gun dealer. So much for my detecting ability.

The policeman actually looked a bit like my father. My father was also tall, with thick hair; the only difference was that my father wore glasses.

I'm sure I've mentioned that my father and I don't see eye to eye. The last thing I needed was a cop who looked like him. I was likely to antagonize him just because he looked like a parent. I stood up to shake his hand, careful to keep my face neutral.

He said, "No, ma'am, please, finish your snack, we have plenty of time. Name's Sergeant Canfield. Russell Canfield. Friends call me Russ."

In spite of his similarity to my father in looks, he was much nicer to me than my father had ever been. My father would have said, "What are you doing, eating at this time of day? You'll ruin your dinner. Come on, let's go." It wouldn't matter that I didn't eat since 9:30 this morning.

I shook his hand and sat down again to my meal. "I'm d'Arcy Carter."

Peyton introduced himself, then indicated a dining room chair for the sergeant and another for the antiques dealer. "D'Arcy, this is Mr. Walker, the antiques dealer who has expressed an interest in the rifles we found upstairs."

I cleared my mouth of oatmeal and waved my spoon. "Nice to meet you. Please excuse me eating in your presence. I work odd hours, and this is the first time since this morning I've had a chance to eat. Do you want anything? Water, crackers, oatmeal?"

Both men shook their heads. "So, where do you work?" Russ asked.

"Uh, Nouveau Deli, in a manner of speaking."

"Oh, Nouveau Deli. Big doings over there the other day," Russ said.

I nodded. "Are you the sergeant in charge of the case?"

Russ laughed. "Oh, no, that's not how it works. That's Dearborn's jurisdiction."

"And you're a sergeant for Romulus."

"Right. Besides, I'm just a patrolman. I do some desk work because I'm a sergeant, but I don't get involved in possible wrongful death."

"That would go to—"

"Homicide. Dearborn PD."

"Do they think it's a homicide?"

"Hey, how would I know?"

"I know, you're not in the Dearborn police department."

The light from my chandelier twinkled in his eyes. "You seem to be more than a little interested in this case, yourself, ma'am. May I ask why?"

I finished the bowl of oatmeal, licking the spoon in thought. Finally, making my decision, I said, "I'll level with you, Sergeant. I was hired at Nouveau Deli to investigate a sabotage case. It may be related to Charlie's death."

"I see. Well, now, I do happen to be good friends with the homicide detective on the case."

"You are? Good. Can you pass my name on to him? I might have some information that's helpful."

"If you plan to cooperate with her, sure, I'll do that." He emphasized the word 'her,' and I suddenly understood why he'd been so coy about the information he was giving out.

"Chances are, she'll find my name out, anyway," I said, not elaborating on why I thought that.

I wrote my name down on a sheet of paper and handed it to Sergeant Canfield as Mr. Walker clasped and unclasped his hands. "Someone died at Nouveau Deli?" he asked.

"A manager," I said. "The deli was open again today."

"That's awful. I hadn't heard. Was it in the papers or on the news?"

I shrugged. "I don't read the papers often."

To change the subject, Peyton said, "Well, the rifles are upstairs. Uh, none of them are loaded," he said as he noticed Mr. Walker blanching. "Please watch your step. We're renovating." He opened the door to the attic and led us up the stairs.

The rifles sat, neatly stacked along the untorn wall in the front of the house. Sergeant Canfield knelt down by them. He began his search over the rifle stocks, looking for identifying marks, writing anything unusual down on a steno pad.

A few had registration numbers or similar markings, but two seemed unmarked. "These may have been hand made and never registered," Sergeant Canfield said. "I'm writing down all the different markings, just to make sure they weren't identified as being used in a crime."

Meanwhile, Mr. Walker studied the rifles after Canfield was done. Every once in a while, I heard him murmuring, and occasionally, I heard an "mmm" or an "aah," but he said nothing out loud.

"You haven't actually seen these yet?" I asked Mr. Walker. I looked over at Peyton.

"Peyton brought two with him the other day," Mr. Walker answered. "The .276 Pederson and the Browning Over and Under 'Grand Luxe.' They're very good rifles."

Once Sergeant Canfield was done, he turned to Peyton. "Which of you found the rifles?"

Peyton said, "I did."

"Where?"

Peyton pointed to the space where he'd torn the wall panelling down. "They were behind there. I found them when I was getting rid of it to enlarge this space."

"So you're saying whoever emplaced the panelling just built it around the rifle stocks?"

"Yessir."

"No openings into the hole of any kind."

"Not that I saw. Well, there were two layers of panelling, actually. Maybe the first one had a door that the second person didn't notice when he put up the second set of panelling."

Canfield looked at me, and I shook my head. "I never noticed an entrance."

"How old is the panelling?"

"Well," I said, closing my eyes to remember what I knew, "The house was built in 1940, and from what the previous owner knew, the attic here was left unfinished. He thought someone put up the panelling in the late forties, maybe early fifties, in an aborted attempt to finish the space. He found a cancelled employee check tucked into a rafter in the basement, and figured it might have been the one used to fix up the place. Vernon Blake's check, I think."

"What is the previous owner's name?"

"Leon Finley. But he went to a nursing home, Ypsi Estates, and died a year later. Maybe he had relatives, but I wouldn't swear to it."

Sergeant Canfield nodded, writing in his book. "Do you know when he moved in here?"

"Some time in the fifties, I'd say."

"Well, great. You've been a big help. I'll see if we can clear these rifles for you so you can sell them." He turned to Walker. "You ready to go?"

Walker stood up from a kneeling position, banging his head on the low ceiling as he did so. "Yes. I want your rifles, Peyton. Looks like you've got $20,000 worth of rifles and shotguns here. Those—" He pointed to the two polished pieces Canfield had said may be hand made. "Those are worth fifty five hundred or so."

"Oh?" I said. "Why?"

"If I'm recognizing the markings, and I think I am, that's a Browning Midas Grade Over/Under with a vent rib. Very rare, very well made."

"How do you know this?"

"I've got a recent MODERN GUN VALUES, from GUN DIGEST. You might want to get a copy for yourself, so you know what kind of money you should you be getting for each gun."

"Thanks for the information. We'll get in touch with you as soon as we know if we can sell them."

Peyton led them back downstairs. He palmed the edge above the door as he went through the downstairs opening.

We made some pleasantries with the two men, who then went off to do their respective jobs. Peyton turned to me when they were gone and shouted, "Woman, you got a gold mine in your attic!"

"Let's hope they can be sold, shall we?"

CHAPTER 18
"A Possible Buyer"

I knocked on the door to Cille's small house. Cille lived in Wayne, the next town over from Romulus. Her house was at the end of a cul-de-sac on the outskirts of her town, close to the outskirts of my town, about a mile from Jennifer's place.

She lived alone, in a house that was reminiscent of an English cottage, both inside and out. In spite of the fact that Cille would never make a fortune at Nouveau Deli, she lived frugally, and as far as I could tell, relatively well.

Cille had window boxes filled with deep purple and pink petunias and bright yellow zinnias. The boxes were painted white to match the rest of the trim, the house itself a putty colored stucco.

She opened the door after my second knock. Her eyes were red, probably from crying, and I realized she still mourned the loss of Charlie. She'd been one of the few who could get along amicably with the late personnel/dining room manager.

She opened the door wider when she realized who it was,

and allowed me to bring in my bicycle. In spite of the quaint-
ness of her own little home, Cille lived, as I did, in a rough
section of town. She, personally, had had a bicycle stolen right
outside her door, so she always let me store my bike inside.

After I parked the bike by her hall closet, I lifted my wool
and pattern book out of the saddle bag basket. "How are you
holding up, Cille?"

"Oh, d'Arcy, it's been just awful. I can't believe this
happened. If I'd only known—" She broke off. "But none of
us could have known, could we? Would you like a drink?"

"Iced tea would be great."

Cille made the greatest iced tea in the world, a mixture of
her own mint and chamomile. She poured me a tall glass, a
glass she had made from an old coke bottle. Cille was big on
recycling, and had been since the early seventies.

We both took our drinks and went to sit on her couch.
Cille's recycling fetish extended to clothing. She'd made several quilts from clothing she outgrew or grew tired of, and they
covered almost everything in her house. A particularly beautiful crazy quilt of pink, green and white lined her couch. I once
heard her call it her late sixties quilt. All of the pieces of clothing came from her high school days.

"I have a video, if you want to watch it, or we can just
talk," she said. She sat down and reached for her knitting, knowing already what my answer would be.

It looked to me as though Cille was still working on the
same piece she'd been knitting in May, when I last came to her
house. "Is that the same Donegal tweed?" I asked, reaching
out to touch the scratchy gray yarn that had slubs of turquoise
and green spattered through it.

"Yeah, I don't knit much in the summer. It gets too hot to
hold the wool. But I finished another quilt. I'd show it to you,
but I sent it to St. Vincent DePaul's last week."

I murmured that I would have liked to have seen it. "What
was this about the ribbon yarn?"

"What? Oh, that. I took it back to the store. Decided I

didn't like the colors."

"Hmm." I almost said something about Ralph and Genevieve, but caught myself just in time. "Well, a friend of mine is having a baby, so I thought I'd get started on something for that happy occasion. I just don't know what yet."

I went through the motions of choosing a pattern from the magazine I'd brought with me. Cille settled down to knitting her sleeve. All the while, I tried to think of how to bring up the events going on at the deli. I didn't have to think that hard. Cille started it.

"So, why on earth did you come back, d'Arcy? I thought you made a permanent break from there."

"Yeah, so did I. Money wasn't coming in fast enough, though, and I have a mortgage to pay."

"Hear, hear. That's the main reason I've stayed for so many years. Good news is, though, I'm finally halfway through with the payments on this place."

"You've lived here fifteen years?"

"Yeah." She turned her knitting to begin another row. "Worked five years at the deli, can you imagine?"

I wondered why, after so many years, she didn't have a management job there. "Five years as a supervisor?"

"No, three years as a supervisor. I refused to be one for awhile."

"Oh, why's that?"

"Do you need any more tea, d'Arcy?"

I looked down at my glass, and realized for the first time that it was empty. "No, that's okay. Maybe later. You were saying?"

Cille turned another row. "Oh, it seems silly now. But I was shy, not supervisor material at all. I was content to just do cash and wait on customers."

"Cille, you can't be shy and work at Nouveau Deli. We get a thousand people in there each weekday, for God's sake."

"I told you, it sounds silly now. But back then, there weren't as many guests, and I really was shy. But then, so many supervisors came and went, and some of them were aw-ful--"

"Like me?" I asked, laughing. "Oh, this would be good. A blanket for the new kid. What do you think?"

Cille nodded at the aran style blanket I showed her. "Very nice. Oh, you're not a bad supervisor, d'Arcy. You're just rela-tively new. It takes time till it's second nature. It took me almost a year and a half before I felt comfortable suping."

She stood up, took my glass and hers, and refilled them in the kitchen. I cast on 177 stitches. "Did you know, I actually began working there before Charlie did?"

"No. I thought Charlie was there from the start. Six years ago."

"Oh, that's, I mean, that was his story. Fact is, he was hired two months after me. I taught him how to take orders, I showed him how to do cash."

"Why didn't you get that managership, then?"

Cille didn't answer for a long time. She knitted two com-plete rows. I finished one row, establishing the complicated cable and moss stitch pattern. When she finally answered, I'd almost forgotten my question. "I was stupid," she said. "I could've had that managership. I would've done a better job of it. Charlie, God rest his soul, was so disorganized and, well, inept at the job."

"Well—"

"God, d'Arcy, wasn't it terrible that he died? I never ex-pected that. I can't get over it."

"Well, I didn't want him dead, either, but maybe now's your chance. You could be the next personnel/dining room manager." I stroked her arm to comfort her.

"Yeah, right," she said, tears glistening in her eyes. "This is not how I wanted it to be. Poor Charlie."

She started to rock back and forth on the couch, dropping her knitting into her lap. There was nothing I could do to as-suage her grief.

After awhile, I picked up my knitting and knit one row.

To change the subject, I said, "You wouldn't believe what I found in my attic, Cille."

Cille mopped her face with the back of her hand. "What?"

"Ten rifles. The antiques dealer says they're worth something."

"Really. Rifles? What kind?"

"I don't know. He said there was a Pederson something, a few Brownings—"

"Any Winchesters?"

"Winchesters? I don't know. Yeah, I think so. Cille, I didn't know you knew anything about guns."

"Then I must have never shown you my collection." She put down her knitting and stood up. "Here, I'll show them to you now."

I followed her to her spare room. She opened the door and I saw the gun rack immediately. The guns were in good shape, I could see that from the other side of the room.

"I collect Winchesters, see," she said. "I'm looking for a .44 Hotchkiss Model 1883 with the tubular magazine. So if you have one—"

"Wait, wait, you're talking Greek to me. What the hell is a tubular magazine?"

Cille picked up one of the rifles and showed it to me as she described it. "This is a Model 1886, a lever action repeating rifle. This here is a tubular magazine." She pointed to the stock of the rifle, then pulled out the magazine. "This, in case you didn't know, carries the bullets."

"Okay."

"It's got a half-octagon rear site, here, and a bead front. They stopped making this rifle in 1939. By the way, I wouldn't mind an 1886 Carbine, either. Looks exactly like this rifle, but it has a 22 inch barrel instead of the 26 inch, like this. But it's very rare, I'm sure you probably don't have one of those."

"Well, I'll look, but to be honest, I'm not even sure I can sell them. They may have been stolen."

"Really? That's kind of interesting." Suddenly, Cille became very serious. "You know, Charlie collected rifles, too. Just one more thing we had in common."

I couldn't stop her as she started to cry.

CHAPTER 19
"Joe Shows his True Colors"

During the night, clouds rolled in, along with at least three spectacular thunderstorms, and the day dawned cold and wet. It was the kind of day when I don't like getting out of bed.

I lay there, dozing, thinking how nice it would be to just laze in bed all day rather than waking at five, going to the deli, getting soaked on the bicycle and sniffling once I got there.

But I don't work at the deli anymore, I can sleep in. I turned over, set to go back to sleep. Then my eyes opened wide. Yes, I did work at the deli. What was my schedule?

I sat up, clearing any fog from my brain, and remembered Thursday was my day off. Phew. I lay back down. But it wasn't really a day off, since I was working on a case.

Thursday. Oh, yes. An interview at eight a.m. with Joe from Joe's Cafe.

Still no need to get up at five a.m. I checked the alarm to make sure I'd set it for about six thirty, then went back to sleep.

Waking up in the middle of the night like that, panicking

that I was due at the deli, was one of the myriad reasons, unrelated to my hatred of Charlie, for why I'd left. I am not a morning person. I never have been. In college, I scheduled all my classes for eleven a.m. or after.

Somehow I'd ended up being a morning opener at the deli. They'd needed morning openers when I interviewed, and I'd made the mistake of saying, sure, I could do that.

What I didn't realize was that because a deli's biggest money comes from lunch, I ended up eating breakfast at five, lunch at nine, and then I'd go without food till after three. It wreaked havoc with my bodybuilding diet, among other things. At three thirty, I was usually willing to eat anything. Heaven help me if the first thing I saw was a donut.

I woke again at six thirty a.m., and listened to the rain hitting my windows with delicate pings. Reaching over, I pulled up my window blind and watched. I could barely see the rain. It was a fine mist, which watered the non- existent garden and caressed my window. I imagined Cille's petunias and zinnias under my window, and laughed. My black thumb would have a heyday.

Fighting the urge to once again get back into my bed, I got up and took a shower. Peyton had already gone to classes at Eastern Michigan University. Seemed pretty early to me, but then, it was a thirty to forty-five minute drive, depending on traffic, and he'd been stupid enough to schedule an eight o'clock class. He'd left me a note on the dining room table to let me know when he'd be back.

I ate my favorite breakfast of oatmeal, then heated up a mug of leftover coffee. I settled down on the living room couch with my small notebook, to write down some questions I wanted to ask Joe.

First, though, I let the cheery yellow, white and black of the room overwhelm me as I tried to get into a good frame of mind. I'm not a natural fan of yellow, but when I came home one day and saw what Peyton had created, I had to say I adored it. In a room, the color could be elegant and cheerful.

One might have thought the black and white barber pole stripes and zebra-style area rug would be too busy, but the actual result was refreshing and friendly.

Not conducive to working, though, I decided as I finally took my last sip of coffee and stared at the empty page.

To make it look as though I were really doing an article for the newspaper, I would have to ask some newspapery questions. His full name, where he went to school, what he did before he got involved in deli life.

How did he get the idea to create this deli, and how did he choose the actual site? This was actually a loaded question. I wanted to know that answer, whereas the rest was just cover work.

I wanted to convince him to give me a tour. I wanted to interview some of his employees, to see if I could get a slip about espionage somewhere.

I wanted to get his take on Charlie's death, which I might be able to do if I worked it in to the conversation delicately.

At seven thirty, I was ready to go. I had my list of questions. I was dressed in jeans and an Irish fisherman's sweater, plus a forest green slicker and gum boots. I covered my bike as well as I could with plastic. Time to venture out in the rain.

The ride to Joe's Cafe is similar to that of Nouveau Deli. Go up Middle Belt Road, which, because of the nasty construction on I-94 around the exit, was less used nowadays.

It was kind of fun to pedal right up the middle of the road, not having to worry about impatient drivers swerving around me and blaring their horn. If there's one thing that always unnerved me on a bike, it's when the driver behind me decided he had to let me know he existed. As though the sound of the engine didn't give it away. A horn never sounded as loud to the driver as it did to the poor biker. It sounded like an explosion.

Turn right on Michigan Avenue, by Hughes Investigations, and pedal one mile to Joe's.

I parked and locked my bike in front of the building, on the porch of the two-floor storefront that had been turned into a restaurant. Then I went inside.

It was like a ghost town. I'd have to agree with Joe that this was his least busy time. There was no one here. At first, I couldn't even find someone working there.

Finally a young girl with a blond pony tail came bouncing back from the sandwich making area. "Yes?" she said, her face barely cracking a smile.

"I have an appointment with Joe. Is he here?"

"Yeah, hold on." She picked up the phone, turned it on to deli-wide page, and shouted, "Joe, your appointment's here." It came out muffled, sounding like, "Yo yo appoymenz ear."

"He should be down any second," she said, presumably to me, although she'd ducked her head into the salad case.

"May I have something to drink while I'm waiting?" In the back of my mind, I caught myself thinking that at Nouveau Deli I wouldn't have had to ask; the workers were told to suggest a drink. What a cult that place was—I caught myself thinking how much better it was than any other place, and yet I knew I didn't believe it.

Nouveau Deli had its share of problems. As Cille had mentioned last night. Charlie was not a good manager, yet he had been in charge of personnel, training, and the goings-on behind the counter, the sandwich making area and the dining room. Just before I'd left in May, not enough workers had been hired, and rumor had it Charlie was reining in labor expenses to help pay for an expansion.

Our, I mean, Nouveau Deli's building was not big enough to seat the two thousand or more people who came in every weekend, most of them at lunchtime. Getting the money to expand by tightening the labor situation, though, was backasswards, as far as I was concerned. If we couldn't treat the customers right because we were stretched too far, we'd lose them instead of gaining them. Right?

I shook these thoughts from my mind and paid for a Diet

Coke, then sat down at one of the tables in the dining area. I was not being paid to tell Sid how to run his business, after all.

Joe took his own time coming down to meet me. I'd begun to wonder if maybe he hadn't heard the page, and I stood up to re-alert the waitperson. Just then, an old looking man wearing a ketchup and corned beef stained full-length apron walked into the room from behind one of the counters. The look of his apron made my stomach do a back flip. I was glad it wasn't two days ago when I had my hangover, or I might have thrown up.

"Are you Joe?" I asked, and the man nodded as he slipped into the chair opposite where I'd been sitting. I sat, too, and as I did so, he stood up.

"Want something to drink? I'm diabetic, so I'm always thirsty," he said. His voice was gruff and had a slight wheeze, as though besides having diabetes, he smoked.

He went over to the pop fountain and poured a large Coke for himself. I shook my head, indicating my diet pop. I guessed him to be around sixty or so. I was kind of assuming he looked older than he was, since he looked, like, eighty. His stained t-shirt bulged over his belly and tucked into loose fitting jeans, barely held up by a worn leather belt. His hair was wavy and thick, mostly white with a touch of gray.

He sat again. His foray to the pop machine had winded him, and so he gasped for a minute before he said, "So what's this article about?"

"Well, a feature article on you, and your deli."

"Not a review, eh, too bad, we got great food." He spoke with machine gun speed, making me think he must originally have come from New York.

"Well, of course, we'll cover some of what you serve, but we were interested in knowing more about you, and how you set up shop here. Sort of so the readers of the *Detroit News* know why you're so popular around here." I refrained from looking around at the obviously popular empty deli this morning. "Shall we get started?"

He nodded, picking an ice cube out of his drink and sucking on it with reddened fingers, stained by pastrami blood.

I tore my eyes away from his hands and looked instead at his face. "So where do you come from originally?"

"What, you can't tell? Manhattan. Lower East Side. Delancey Street. And no, I wasn't a pickle vendor." He laughed as though I should understand his joke, and broke off with a wheeze.

"My father worked in a delicatessen, and his father before him. Before that, my mama's family was deli owners in Poland, my father's side, Italian restaurants. Not like those fakers at Nouveau Deli." He pronounced the name with emphasis on the 'new'.

"Do I sense some resentment here?"

He looked up from his second ice cube, then popped it into his mouth. "No, no, nothing like that. Nah, they're just the primary competition, like they say in the restaurant biz. Except, because of them, I can't run a deli like I would. I would sell meats by the pound, and cheeses, little in the way of the sandwich and drink and salad line."

"Why'd you choose the name of Joe's Cafe?" I pretended to write interested notes, but so far, I'd only written 'instant antagonism toward n.d.', plus a few stars and other jagged doodles across the page. A guy I once dated told me stars and jags meant I was sexually repressed. That was probably true.

"That's exactly what I'm saying. It would've been Joe's Deli, except there was another deli down the street. And because they had sandwiches, everybody expected me to have sandwiches. So I made myself different by adding my own bakery. And God damn it, they had to add baked goods to their line."

I wrote it all down diligently as though that were a great quote, all the while thinking I'd been told Nouveau Deli'd had baked goods there before Joe's Cafe was a twinkle in Joe's eye. Which was the true story? "I didn't catch your full name, Joe. Can you spell it?"

"Canelli. Like the dessert, only different." He laughed at his own joke again, then spelled the name for me. Dutifully, I wrote it down. Maybe I could get Ralph to look up his name and see if he had a record or something in Manhatten before he came here.

"Why'd you settle down in Michigan?"

"My wife's a Michigander. She liked her town, her mother's sick. So I moved out here. New York's filled with delis, but here? Almost none to speak of. Only Zingerman's in Ann Arbor, Nouveau Deli, and then us. The others are just sandwich shops calling themselves delis. Now, you ask me, Zingerman's is a good deli. Like I'd try to do."

"How'd you choose Dearborn?"

"What's not to like about Dearborn? The Ford headquarters, we get a lot of biz from them. And my wife can go to the nursing home easy from here."

"So she works at the nursing home?"

"Nah, works here with me. You just missed her. Got a telephone call; mother's worse." He sucked down the last of his ice from his paper Coke cup. "You must not eat here often, you don't know her."

"I'm sorry to hear that," I said, actually in reference to the mother-in-law.

"Eh." He waved away the comment with his hand, and stood up to get himself another drink.

When he sat down again, I said, "Water would probably be better for you."

"You're just like my wife. So, you got enough info for your article there?" Joe pulled a small knife out of his pocket and cleaned the underside of his nails with it.

"I was hoping I could take a tour of the deli. We'll be having photographers here, after all, so I need to find the best pictures."

"Well, I can take you for a short tour. Ten minutes, no longer. I got work to do, you know."

I nodded, stood up to show him I'd waste no time. I followed him as he showed me around, starting at the main ordering and dining area. He didn't point out anything I hadn't noticed before.

Without speaking, he took me to the bakery. There, two people stood, smoking and joking. Again, my stomach turned. It was a serious health code violation to smoke in a food preparation area. Yet here, both bakers did so.

"You allow smoking here?"

"What are you, health department? If so, you got the wrong deli. You hear about the Nouveau? I hear one them managers kicked it two days ago. Food poisoning."

"Where'd you hear that?"

"Look, food industry, you hear all the good dirt. Bad dirt, too, as the case may be. Boy, were they asking for that, too."

"Definitely food poisoning?" He nodded. I took a note again. I wanted to know who'd told Joe Canelli about Nouveau Deli's woes. Did we have a leak? There I went, thinking "we" yet again. Nouveau Deli, the cult.

"So, you think they've got bad health violations there?"

"I'm telling you, they've paid the health department off, that's what I'm telling you."

"Who told you that?"

"I got my sources."

"Well, I see that. But if you can't tell me where the source comes from, I can't use it in my article."

That stopped him. Obviously, he hadn't thought of the angle the media could play with this little tidbit of information. I could see him being tempted by what I could do for him as a newspaper reporter.

"Well, I can't divulge my sources, you understand, but I'll tell you this. There's dissension in the ranks there, and the one planning to leave a sinking ship had a lover in the health department. So I hear."

Lynnette was cheating on Sid, and getting carte blanche from the health department? That was hard for me to believe. Lynnette seemed much too straight to do that. In fact, I'd call her a bit of a prude. She was the one who stressed to us the importance of hygiene and sanitation.

Which brought me to another thing. The fact was, Nouveau Deli scored high on health inspections because they were clean and they deserved the high marks. I wondered if I could find out what Joe's Cafe had gotten. Personally, I'd seen several critical violations that were technically bad enough to close them down. So, who was paying the health department off?

CHAPTER 20
"Lifting Names"

I didn't say any of that to Joe, however. I just nodded, took a note, and then followed him through the kitchens, where one person did not stop chopping his vegetables even as he looked sullenly at me. Hoping he wouldn't chop off a finger in my presence, I hurried out of the area.

Joe took me on a short tour of the office upstairs, and then told me he'd have to get back to work. "Got a lot of food ordering to do," he said as he showed me to the stairs, expecting me to find my own way out.

As soon as I was out of his eyesight, I had an idea. I stepped as obviously as possible down to the bottom of the stairs. While I did this, I took note of any creaky boards in the staircase. Thus, when I crept back up to the middle landing, I made no noise. Located in this cramped area was the time clock and all the time cards of the employees. There were only twenty of them, compared to Nouveau Deli's seventy or more. I thanked my lucky stars, then wrote down every name and social security number as quickly as I could. I abbreviated many of the names to keep from being caught in the act.

When I was done, I snuck back down the stairs and exited through the back door.

Rotting lettuce, carrots, and hunks of what must once have been pastrami lay in piles where they'd missed the dumpsters. What a stench. I was willing to bet they never bothered to hose the area down. Three years of decay lay at my feet. It was pretty disgusting, I had to admit, even with my biased reaction.

I picked my way through the debris, holding my breath until I'd reached the corner of the alley. Then I jogged back to my bike and hopped on.

The rain had stopped while I was inside, but the sky still looked threatening. Overall gray sky bore pockmarks of dark gray clouds floating close to the earth. I didn't bother to unwrap my bike.

I checked my watch. Nearly 10:00. I had just enough time to ride down to the church for Charlie's funeral. I didn't want to go, but felt I had to.

Slowly, I pedalled there, locked the bike and went in. About fifty people sat in the pews. I recognized the backs of some of the heads in front of me. Karen sat in the front row, Sid behind her about two rows back. Lynnette sat with him but two feet down the pew. Cille and Jennifer sat together a few rows in front of me.

So who was running the deli, I thought, but then reminded myself of the fifty other people who worked at the restaurant.

The memorial service only took about twenty minutes. Charlie had been cremated, so we didn't have to view the body or go to the cemetery, two facts which made me truly grateful. I hugged Karen and gave her my condolences again. She looked as though she hadn't taken a Valium today; she'd been crying, as evidenced by her red-rimmed eyes.

After the funeral, I rode back down Michigan Avenue to my new place of work, the Hughes Investigations office.

Genevieve must have seen me come up. She jumped from

her seat and opened the door for me. "Come on in and bring your bike with you. It's going to storm like crazy."

"Thanks. How are you doing today?"

"Not bad." Her eyes blinked a few times. "I'm a grandmother!"

"That's terrific. Boy or girl?"

"Little girl. Name's Ann Marie, just like her great grandmother."

"How's the sweater?"

"Oh," she said. She sat down with a huff. "I've only got the back and one sleeve done. But I'm knitting it two hours a day, so I hope it'll be done as a christening present."

"Good luck. If you need any help, let me know."

She pulled out a magazine from her knitting drawer. "Look what I bought today during my lunch hour." She showed it to me.

It was a knitting magazine filled with cute designs for children of all ages. As I paged through the pictures, I paused at an adorable red sweater covered with Scottie dogs. "Isn't that cute?"

"I can make something for her every year with this thing."

"New grandma plans to be busy. I bet Ralph is thrilled."

"Oh, Ralph is Ralph. I bet he's thrilled, too, but tell us?" She laughed.

I walked into the back room. A hint of envy rose and fell around inside my brain. I knew Genevieve was so happy about her new grandchild. I wondered to myself how my parents would react if I ever had a child. Not half so thrilled, I'd bet. With my luck, I'd be a single mother, and I'd be disinherited, again, my child along with me.

I surprised Ralph as he opened the bathroom door and banged it into the door I'd just opened.

"Sorry."

"Hi, d'Arcy. I'm sure you heard Genevieve's all excited."

"Sure. That's great. You happy?"

"I didn't want to be a grandfather so soon, but I'm glad

Heather and Jim had a healthy baby."

"Mm-hmm." Just what Genevieve had said. Ah, to be a man, and have an impenetrable skin to hide behind. Okay, okay, men didn't deserve such generalizations. Just look at my father. He had no trouble showing his complete disdain for me.

Boy, how did I get in such a bad mood? Must have been my interview with Joe. His brusque personality had reminded me of dear old Dad.

He walked back to his desk, pointing to a desk which sat to the right of his. "We just cleaned that out for you, so by the time this case is over, it'll be all ready."

"Thanks."

"So, tell me how it's going."

I told him what I'd learned so far, including what I'd written down in my notebook and what little I'd learned at Joe's Cafe.

"I don't really have any reason to believe he's sabotaging the deli, although he's awfully antagonistic toward them. What I'm more interested in is what he was saying about Lynnette and the health department lover. I don't believe it, but I think I should check into the rumor."

"Just because he doesn't seem the type to sabotage the deli doesn't mean you should get rid of him as a suspect."

"Oh, I'm not. I plan to follow up by checking all his employees against Nouveau Deli's and see if there are any social security numbers that match."

"Good."

"Meanwhile, I wondered if you could check to see whether or not Joe Canelli had a record in New York."

"Very good. You're thinking. I can run that information down for you. Remind me eventually to teach you how to do that for yourself. What else do you have?"

"I've got to talk to Sid about what's going on between him and Lynnette."

"That's what I wanted to hear."

"I checked out Karen, Charlie's wife. I don't think she had anything to do with it. She's barely holding together as it is."

"Well, maybe not, but you should always check that out."

We looked at each other for a moment. Something occurred to me, and I said, "Just on the off chance, why don't you check to see if Ben Mitchell worked in the Health Department."

Ralph looked at me a moment, then laughed. "What an idea. Hang on a second." He picked up the phone, dialed, and waited. "Yeah, sport, how ya doing? Great. Hey, remember that guy I was trying to track down earlier this week? Yeah. Hey, can you find out if he worked for the Health Department?"

Another wait. Ralph said, "He's checking right now. Yeah, Jake? Hmm, okay, thanks."

He hung up. "No dice, I'm afraid. But that was a great hunch. You're doing all right, d'Arcy. This case may seem to be getting more complex as it goes along, but remember that with each clue, the mystery will get closer to becoming clear. That has always happened for me, and I know you'll do it, too."

"Thanks." I stood up to go.

"You don't own a car, do you, d'Arcy?"

"Now, how'd you know that?"

"Two out of three times, you come in here with healthy roses on your cheeks. The only time you didn't, you were in an interview suit. Tousled hair that's slightly scrunched down on the top of your head. I say you borrowed a car for the other occasion. You ride a bike, and I'll bet, like a good girl, you always wear your helmet."

"Yeah, it's true. But I think I'm in the market for a car."

"Probably a good idea in this line of work. Any idea what kind you're looking for?"

"Small, old, good gas mileage, cheap. Preferably foreign. One I can change the rotor on."

"Your wants are few." He laughed, opening the door for me. "I'll keep an eye out for you. A friend of mine has an old Saab he might be willing to give up."

"Saab, huh." I tried to picture a Saab in my head, but had no luck. Too bad. I couldn't see whether I'd look good in a Saab or not.

CHAPTER 21
"What Salad is This?"

The phone was ringing when I entered the living room. I ran to pick it up before Peyton's answering machine did. "Hello?" I yelled into the receiver.

"Hi, did you just come in?"

"Tim, hello."

"How are you, d'Arcy?"

"Oh, I've been pretty busy, what with the deli and everything." I started to twirl the phone cord around my finger, then realized I did that every time I talked to Tim on the phone. I unrolled it, then started trying to straighten the cord into even swirls.

"Look, d'Arcy, are you mad at me?"

"What makes you think that?"

"Well, you haven't called, you turned frosty on me the other night after we—"

"No, I—" What was my problem, anyway? I'd been afraid to call him, of course. Afraid of this moment. But why?

Because I just knew it wouldn't work out. I could feel it in the same way my bones could feel rain before the clouds came. "I don't know how to explain it."

Tim was silent for a moment. Then he said, "Did I go too fast?"

"I shouldn't have gotten drunk. I apologize."

"Is that all, d'Arcy? It's okay, you know. We didn't do anything."

"I didn't black out, Tim. I know what we did and didn't do. I'm just—"

"Embarrassed?"

"Yeah."

"You've no reason to be. I'm the one should be embarrassed."

"Why?"

"It was my idea, wasn't it?"

"Your idea?"

"To go out for drinks."

"Well, yeah." I stopped speaking. That had been the longest conversation we'd been able to sustain since we'd gotten back from Grayling. But how long would it last?

"How 'bout Friday night?" he asked.

"Excuse me?"

"One day from now, evening."

"Yes, that's Friday, isn't it? I don't drink much."

"No drinks, I promise. Barbecue at my place."

"I don't know, Tim." I wiped the sweat from my forehead. Was it from the ride or the phone call? Probably both.

"Look, some buddies from work will be here. You don't have to be here alone with me."

"That's not what I'm trying to say."

"Then what is it you're trying to say? Don't back away from me now, d'Arcy."

"I'm not."

"You are. Why? If you don't like spending time with me, let me know that now. I'm an adult, I can take it."

Oh, Tim, it's not you, I thought. It's men. I don't know what to do with you or with any of the men in my life. "I—uh, what time?"

"Then you'll come."

I sighed. "I'll try. This thing at the deli is really heating up."

"Well, yeah, I can see that. The paper's been covering some of it. Anything I can do to help you out?"

"Well, just bring your rally driving skills around, and we'll...That was a joke. Oh, never mind." He probably wouldn't even remember the time we went bahaing in the woods around Grayling. Shut up, d'Arcy. "I'll let you know if there is. Not right now, as far as I can tell."

"Make it seven o'clock. And, d'Arcy?"

"Yeah."

"Why don't you bring Peyton? There's a great lawyer I think he'd like to meet."

"Okay." I hung up, wanting to cry. What on earth had I been trying to say there? I'd ended up sounding like an idiot. I pushed it out of my mind. It wouldn't help to think about it. Then I laughed, as a random thought came to my mind. Did Tim plan to introduce Peyton to a male or female?

I realized my hands were shaking. I poured myself a cup of coffee, but then decided I didn't want it. I left it on the counter and walked into the bedroom. Maybe I just needed a nap.

As I lay looking up at the ceiling, I tried to keep my mind on the case. Much as letting my mind just wander would prob-ably help me sort out some things that weren't coming together, my emotions couldn't afford that kind of meandering. No tell-ing what my brain would dredge up.

After about fifteen minutes I was on the edge of sleep. Images were coming to me fast and furious. White flashes, a face, Jeremy? No, I knew better. More flashes. Jennifer, Cille, Sid, Ralph, Tim.

Tim. What was it I wasn't facing? Would he leave me

like all my lovers before him? Like Jeremy. Of course he would.

This is what I'd been trying to avoid. I shook myself, turned on my side, and began to rock back and forth, hugging myself with my arms. I was awake again.

The salad case appeared in my mind, in sharp focus, then faded into the trash dumped behind Joe's Cafe. I caught a whiff of rotting food, and then soft slumber welcomed me.

I woke the next morning, hunger gnawing at my chest. Before my shower, I devoured a cup and a half of mini wheat biscuits to stop my stomach from eating itself.

I'd gone to bed for a nap, and never gotten up. Peyton hadn't awakened me when he came in. So much for that day. I was back to what I'd done for a year at Nouveau Deli. Go to work, work out, come home and go to bed. Just in time to do it all over again. I hated this job.

How did people like Cille and Jennifer and Sid do this for a living, and worse, seem to enjoy doing it? Nouveau Deli had been a stop-gap for me. A job to have while I looked for a real job, a job that made more than ten thousand dollars a year.

All my jobs had been stop-gap jobs, come to think of it. Would private detective work be the same?

My partners today were Jennifer and Cille. Jennifer did not speak to me as she counted her drawer and set out her baked goods. Cille also was silent. Great. I hadn't been back a week, and already everyone I worked with either hated or distrusted me.

I sent Jennifer on her break first, then considered sending Cille at the same time. Most of my prep was done and there were hardly any customers.

The food poisoning scare had definitely not been kept a secret after Charlie died. No one but no one was coming to Nouveau Deli.

"Was yesterday this quiet?" I asked Cille.

She merely nodded. "Why don't I get another cheese cake? We have to replace the ones that were moldy this morning."

I looked into the dessert case and saw that, as usual, Cille had caught me again. There were only six slices of cheesecake in the case. Even on a slow day, that wouldn't be enough. "Yeah, go ahead, get one from the fridge."

She left, leaving me alone on the line. Not even a customer nearby. I'd never seen such a string of dead days at the deli, not even in the deadest days of January and February.

I bent down through the case windows and stirred the salads, since I could think of no other prep work to do. It was then that I first caught a whiff of food that smelled off. I sniffed every salad in the case. I remembered putting every one of them in, and I'd personally taste-tested each. I couldn't trace the scent to anything in there.

Maybe it was the case drain, backed up because food had fallen into the case and gotten stuck in the pipes. Checking to make sure no customers had come in, I knelt down and checked under the case, expecting to see a pool of stagnant water.

Nothing. I was about to get up when I decided to look again. What was that shiny rectangle I'd seen at the other corner of the salad case?

It was under the left hand side. At first, I thought part of the case undercarriage had fallen. But when I looked the second time, I realized it was a salad pan, wedged in there near the wheel.

Checking one more time to make sure no one else was around, I reached for the pan handle and pulled it out. To my surprise, the pan was full. It contained something that was already in the case. Linda May's smoked salmon hash.

Movement down the hall near the freezers told me Cille was on her way back. I shoved the pan under the case and stood back up again. I stepped over to the popcase to pull out the sour cream, since we'd need that to top the cheesecake.

I had to think.

"Here you go," Cille said.

"What an idiot I am. I should have told you to get more sour cream while you were out there."

"I can go back."

"Never mind, I'll do it. Why don't you get your break ready, and you can take it when I get back?"

She nodded. I went to the fridge for a new tub of sour cream.

So that's how it had been happening.

Hide a salad in a warm place, maybe three hours, and then put it in the case. Just wait for someone to eat it. But something wasn't quite jelling.

This was a salad that didn't sell quickly, one that was tasted every shift change, and would be caught by an unsuspecting shift supervisor. Come to think of it, so was the ham potato salad. What was really going on here?

If you want to actually make someone sick, choose something popular, like Mom's potato salad. Customers would drop like flies.

Whoever was doing this didn't want someone to get sick. They just wanted incredibly high food loss. Judging by the ones that had gone bad, the perpetrator was choosing the most expensive, and least likely to be quickly sold, salads in the deli.

Another thought came into my mind. Charlie's death had been a complete accident. And so had Ben Mitchell's. They'd both been unlucky enough to eat salads that weren't meant to be sold. They'd eaten from them before a shift change, before they'd been quality-checked by anyone.

If I could catch when this salad went into the case, I might be able to figure out who was doing this.

CHAPTER 22
"Down for the Count"

It was nearly 11:30 when Cille got sick. I'd just turned to ask her a question, but stopped when I noticed the white pallor of her skin and the green tinge that had taken the place of her natural blush. "Cille? Are you all right?"

She turned abruptly, and rushed back to the office area. I looked over at Jennifer, who hadn't noticed. She was waiting on a customer. With a rush, I bent down to look under the salad case.

The silver pan under there was gone.

How had whoever had done this get that pan into the case without my noticing? The answer came to me almost immediately. They'd done it while I was on my break. That had been at nine o'clock.

I opened the case and pulled out the offending salad, weighed it out and dumped it without even tasting it. $105 worth of food loss, I might add.

When Jennifer was finished with her customer, I asked

her, "Did you see anyone go into this case while I was on break?"

She opened her till, ostensibly to straighten her twenties. "No."

I knew as soon as she said it that she was lying. I'm not sure how. Maybe it was the fact that she refused to look at me. Could she have done it? If she hadn't, who was she trying to protect?

When there was a break in customers, I walked over to her cash stand. "Jennifer, I need your help. Cille just got sick. She's still in the bathroom. We've got to get to the bottom of this before someone else is killed."

"Lay off it, d'Arcy. We didn't have a problem before you came back."

"What the hell do you mean? What about the food loss?" The words were out before I'd even cleared them with my brain. Be careful, or your cover is blown. She's just throwing you off, blaming you for something she and you both know isn't your fault.

"What?" She said, looking at me with renewed interest. "What food loss?"

"Sid told me when I came back that there'd been a lot of food loss in the last six weeks. He stressed his stupid waste loss management program more than usual."

"You have a customer," she said, pointing to the counter. "Work first, gossip later."

I went back to my station as Cille came back into the deli, looking paler than before. "Are you okay?" I asked as I picked up my order pad.

She nodded, weakly, then walked up to her cash register.

"Why don't you go on home? We can make it without you."

She shook her head, then doubled over with pain. I took the customer's order quickly, then pointed him toward Jennifer, hoping I'd succeeded in distracting his attention from Cille. Then I walked over to her. "Come on, Cille, you're not a good advertisement for the deli in this condition. You look like shit."

"Thanks." She smiled, but just barely. "Yeah, maybe I will go home. I don't know what's wrong."

"What did you eat on break?"

She looked up sharply, her face pinched with pain. "Why?"

"I suspect whatever you ate was laced with salmonella. You may have food poisoning. I need to know what you ate so I can pull it from the case."

"No, that can't be."

I nodded. "What did you have to eat?"

Cille doubled over in pain again. "Uh, I ate, God I can hardly remember. Salmon and some potato salad."

"Okay. Look, go on back to the office and tell Sid to take you to the hospital. We've got to get this cleared up. It's gone too far."

She nodded, then hobbled back to the office area again. I took over her place at the pick up cash stand. Jennifer and I took turns taking orders and ringing people up. Thank God it was a slow day.

Much as I enjoyed working with Jennifer, I suspected she had something to do with the food poisoning problem, though I couldn't as yet prove it. If it wasn't her directly, she knew who was doing it. The fact was, she'd been alone on the line for about ten minutes. She came back from break and I went on break before Cille came back.

That was plenty of time to put that salad into the case with no one else seeing her do it. Or she might be protecting someone who'd done it in her presence. But who? Ned? Lynnette?

Cille was the third one to come down with food poisoning, after Charlie and Ben Mitchell. No, that wasn't quite true. Sid had said that one worker in the deli had also come down with food poisoning, but they'd kept that incident quiet.

I had planned to confront Sid about what was going on between him and Lynnette, but he left the deli before I got off the line. Hopefully, he'd taken Cille to the hospital, as I had suggested, but who knew? He may not have wanted to report any more food poisoning incidents. After all, I was pretty sure the health department was keeping very close tabs on what was happening at Nouveau Deli.

I checked in the kitchen on the off chance that Ned was there, and, luck being with me, he was.

"Hey Ned, when do you get off?"

"Half hour."

"Great. Can I talk to you then?"

He looked at me in surprise while he stirred the sauteed red peppers. "I suppose. Why?"

"I'll explain later. Meet me in the office."

I went back there to wait. While there, I spent some time comparing the list of names from Joe's employee list with names on our time cards. Then I went back over the list, comparing social security numbers. Goddamn it, I thought when I was finally through. There wasn't a match on the list anywhere.

I checked my watch. It had been forty five minutes. Had Ned forgotten, or more likely, stood me up? I was about to go out and check when he slammed the door open. "Sorry, I sort of got caught up in something."

"That's okay. Let's go outside so we can speak privately."

I led him out to the farthest picnic table on the patio, and sat down.

He said, "I gotta admit, you got my curiosity up. What's this about?"

"Food poisoning."

Ned collapsed onto the picnic table bench opposite me. "Yeah, it's terrible. And here I am, the new kitchen manager. It sure doesn't look good on my record."

"How do you think I feel? I was on duty both times, too."

"Both times?" Was that a flash of fear in Ned's eyes, or was it my imagination?

"Cille got sick today. What did you think I was talking about?"

"I don't know," he said, almost too quickly. He sighed.

Suddenly I understood. "You know about the other ones, too, don't you?"

He looked up at me, as though trying to judge whose side I was on. Then he said, "Ben Mitchell. And Brian."

Ah, so it had been Brian who'd warned Sid about the possible problem. Yet another fact Sid hadn't bothered to let me in on. "Tell me what you know about Ben."

"What I know, or what I think I know?"

I remained silent. Awkwardly, he went on. "Ben Mitchell was a friend of Sid and Lynnette's. He went to the hospital, what, three weeks ago? Had the flu. And then he died. Couple days later, Sid came to talk to me, panicking. Said Brian had thought he'd gotten food poisoning here, he thought it was tied to our food loss, thought it was food poisoning that got Ben. Thank God the hospital didn't think to check for that. Well, anyway, Sid blamed me at first."

"That sounds like what you know. What is it you think you know?"

He sighed again, wiped his forehead to remove the sweat that had formed there. "God, it's hot out here. One thing I know is, it's not me. I was able to convince him of that."

"How?"

"How? Because when I finish a salad, it goes right into the walk-in. I never let it sit around. I teach the sanitation class, for God's sake. Sid watched me like crazy, couldn't see anything I was doing wrong, and still the food loss continued."

That jived with what I knew already. "And what do you think you know?"

He eyed me a moment. "What's all your interest in this?"

I arched my back. "I told you. I was on shift when these other two things happened. I want to get to the bottom of this."

He wiped his forehead again. "What I think I know is that Ben Mitchell was more than just a friend of Lynnette's."

I looked at him in shock for a moment, then laughed. "So that's why Sid's so edgy about it, huh?"

"As I said, it's what I think I know."

I thought for a moment before I asked, "What did Ben do for a living?"

He shrugged. "Dunno, really. Worked for the government in some capacity. I think. But, he wasn't killed on your shift, why are you so interested?"

I bit my lip. "Look, you've been straight-forward with me, and I appreciate it. I wish I could be the same. I'll tell you when the time's right."

Ben picked up a mustard container, then set it down. "I think I know anyway, but it's cool. I won't tell anyone."

I stood up and left, wondering if Ned really knew, or if he thought he knew.

*   *   *

Where had my time gone? As far as I could recall, I'd done my whole workout, and couldn't remember anything besides the 225 pound bench press. After I finished my workout, I turned my attention to another thing I wanted to think about. Were there any specific similarities in the suspected salads? I washed my hair and scrubbed down my body in the gym shower. Ham potato salad, salmon hash, ham and bean salad, chicken and rice salad in pesto mayonnaise.

So far, the ones I knew were involved were high protein salads, mixed with mayonnaise. Not heavy sellers.

I'd already decided that whoever was doing this didn't mean to poison the customers. Taking this train of thought, I had to also say I believed it was an internal problem rather than an external one.

Joe Canelli would want the food poisonings to be as public as possible, so Nouveau Deli would lose customers and go to his place. He or an accomplice would let Mom's potato salad go bad, I reasoned.

For the most part, I'd removed Joe and his deli mates from consideration. Every lead I'd tried with him had turned up empty.

I couldn't really rule him out completely, since it had been obvious that he was fairly antagonistic toward Nouveau Deli. But I decided to turn my attention elsewhere until Ralph unearthed some information for me. See what kind of shenanigans he might have pulled before he moved to Dearborn.

CHAPTER 23
"Meeting the Motorcycle Gang"

As I got on my bike, I rejoiced in the power of my workout. Nothing like pumping iron to clear my mind and jump start its working capacity.

It was hot as hell today. The shower had lost its cooling effect by the time I reached the construction on Middle Belt Road. Sweat was rolling down my neck and back. My shirt stuck to my chest in the concave area between my breasts. God, when was this heat going to break? This summer was turning into one of the hottest ones I could remember.

I turned right and pedalled down Smith, then turned left, and nearly ran into the back end of a Harley Davidson. Momentarily, I considered turning around and avoiding the tough looking men, but I would have felt stupid. As I tried to decide what to do, the one with his back to me turned back to look at me.

"Howdy, neighbor," he said, smiling to show nicotine stained crooked teeth. "What's your name?"

"D'Arcy. How about you?"

"Name's Chet, nice to meet you. This here's Randy," he said, pointing to the man facing me, also straddling a Harley. "Seen you drive your baby bike past here every once in a while."

I nodded, smiling at the concept of a baby bike that might grow into a big Harley if given enough time and space. Reminded me of a bonsai tree. "Nice to meet you."

The two men nodded back. "Come on by some time, have a beer. Looks like you could stand one right now. Hot as hell on wheels, huh."

"Thanks, but I really should be getting back home."

I waved as I pedalled past. Intrigued by an overheard word, I strained to hear their conversation.

"Here's your present, and here's the other one, to add to the batch."

"Cool."

"Happy Birthday." One of them roared off in the opposite direction. Must have been Randy. Other present, huh. Drugs maybe. I wouldn't be surprised, in a motorcycle gang. Then I laughed. Sometimes I have an overactive, if somewhat biased imagination. They could be nice guys who hung out and drank beer and never touched a drug in their lives. Who was I to say after meeting them once?

I turned the corner and then the other one, and I was at home. A big glass of ice water was coming my way. Hopefully on a tray held out to me as I stepped inside the front door. Failing that, I'd pour one myself. The sky had clouded over, so I brought my bike into the house with me, just in case it rained.

Peyton was right at the door. Alas, no glass of water in his hand. "Got a call from the sergeant who was here the other day. Every one of the guns is clean. We can sell them all."

I was surprised to feel my heart flipping unhappily in its chest. "Hmm. Any interesting tidbits about them? Are they famous in any way?"

"Well, not really. He says they were registered to some guy named Vernon Blake, an avid gun collector as far as the sergeant could tell. Registered the guns, but probably never used them. They're more for collecting than for hunting."

"And he had ten or so guns."

"Yeah. Anyway, he worked for Ford on the line till probably 1952 or thereabouts. Want me to find his death certificate?"

"Oh, Peyton, I don't think that's necessary."

"So we can sell them."

"Great." I left the bike by the door and headed for the kitchen. There was a glass standing on the counter I was pretty sure I'd used this morning for water, so I refilled it from the container in the fridge.

"I talked to Mr. Walker. Said he'd give us a thousand for each rifle except those two fancy ones. Those he said he'd give five grand for the Browning Midas Grade and the Winchester 1886. He thinks he can sell them to a museum."

I gulped the water down, poured myself a second glass. "Winchester? Is it a Carbine?"

"I have no idea. So?"

"So, what?"

"Well I need your go-ahead to sell them. It's your house we found them in."

"So sell them. On second thought, sell the ones worth a thousand. I want to hang on to the others for a little while. I might have another buyer." I thought Cille might want a look.

Peyton bounced out of the kitchen on lightly rolling feet, and headed up the stairs to gather his wares. We were about to become eight thousand dollars richer.

CHAPTER 24
"More than One Investigator"

I caught sight of Sid around 1:30 p.m. the next day, just before my shift was over. The rest of the half hour, I looked back and forth between customers, trying to ensure that he wouldn't leave prior to the end of my shift. He didn't.

After I punched out, I went to the door to his office and knocked. There was a pause, then his tired voice said, "Come on in."

I entered to find him with his head on the desk. At first I thought he was the next food poisoning victim, but when he raised his head to look at me, I could tell he was just extremely tired. He'd probably been losing sleep over this fiasco. I would, too, in his position, just thinking of the possible law suits.

"Hi," I said, and presented him with my bill so far for the week. Last night I'd typed it neatly on Peyton's MacIntosh and printed it out. So far, I'd worked 43.5 hours on the line, and fifteen hours or so off the line, doing extra investigative work. Before taxes and before Ralph's cut, I'd made $1462.50

so far for working on this case. "Just make the check out to Hughes Investigations."

"This isn't working out," Sid said with no preamble. He took the piece of paper from my hand. "I thought you'd be able to figure this out a lot faster. And, now, Charlie's dead, and—"

I was about to lose the case, goddamn it. And by God, I wouldn't let this happen. The tigress in me came out.

"Maybe if you'd been perfectly frank with me when you hired me, I'd have figured this out a lot faster."

"What?"

"Telling me you thought it was Joe's Cafe, so I had to check out that track. And so far, it's a blind alley; no reason to think it's Joe at all."

"I thought—"

"But you failed to mention what's going on with you and Lynnette. You mean to tell me you don't think Lynnette would try to plant some salmonella to put some heat on you so you'd sell the place?"

"I—"

"I know she's done worse in the past, so don't tell me she's not capable of it."

"I didn't think it was important."

"Yeah, well it is important. How 'bout the controversial kitchen manager you placed the day before the food loss began?"

He sat back in his chair, the look on his face revealing shock. "I didn't realize they coincided."

"To the exact date. You don't tell me those things, I have to take time finding them out. And then you put me on the line for forty some hours, so I have very little time to actually investigate. That's why the investigation's taking longer than you wanted it to."

Sid stood up, then sat down again. He wiped off his forehead, which had begun to bead with sweat. "Okay, you're right. There's more to it than I thought."

"Were you going to try to tell me to quit looking into it? You are getting something for your money, you know."

He didn't say anything for nearly a minute. I wasn't sure what his answer would be, but I was beginning to wonder if I even cared. Fire me, please. I decided to call the bluff. "I'll just leave now, after I give you what I've unearthed so far. No skin off my fingers."

He slumped over in his chair. "No. No, I guess not." He pulled out his personal check book and wrote me the check, wrote down the amount in his ledger. Then he handed it to me.

"Would you like a run down on what I've learned so far?" When he nodded, I went on. "As I told you already, I checked on Joe. I met with him, talked to him, and though he's antagonistic toward the deli, he didn't seem bent on sabotaging us."

"Before or after Charlie's death?"

"After."

"He must have been gloating."

"He was. But, judging by the appearance of his place, he personally wouldn't want to frame us with food poisoning, for fear the health department would also check him out."

"Hmm."

"Right. Ralph Hughes is checking to see if he developed a record in New York City before descending into our fair city. I also took down all the names and socials of his workers. Not a single person who works at Joe's also works here, unless they've forged a social security number. Which I doubt. May I sit down?"

"Yeah, sure, sorry." He stood up, cleared a stack of papers from a red painted folding chair, like the ones the customers used in the deli. Their obvious comfort value made customer turnover time fairly short. I sat down as he did.

"So, that path so far has come up empty. Meanwhile, the conversation I overheard with you and Lynnette makes me think I should investigate that area further."

I paused. When Sid volunteered no information on that subject, I went on, resolving to get back to that area shortly.

"Going over the information in the files, I noticed that the beginning of the food poisoning incidents coincided with the time Ned Beyers started as kitchen manager. I figure maybe it could be a disgruntled employee, who thought they should have been the one promoted." I thought about telling him what I knew about the skewed salaries, but then he'd probably ask how I found that information. I decided to drop that for a moment. "Do you have a list of the people who interviewed for that position?"

He nodded.

"You'll have to give me that list. Oh, and by the way, I found the hiding place for the salads."

He looked up, eyes opening noticeably wider. "What?"

"Yeah, the salads are being hidden in a warm spot, and I assume they stay there until they've been in the danger zone at least three hours. That would guarantee that some form of salmonella or staph infection would develop."

"So, you're right. It is internal."

"That's what it looks like to me. I discovered a suspect salad yesterday, and decided to watch to see when it went into the case. Then, Cille got sick yesterday. I missed when the salad went in."

"Shit."

"Yeah. Meanwhile, I think both Cille and Jennifer have decided I'm the one to blame for the food poisoning, since the ones they know about began after I came back. And I had the motive."

He leaned forward in his chair. "So, are you the one who's doing it?"

I sat up straight.

"Sid, I'd be happy to leave any time. You were the one who asked me back in the first place. You tell me to leave, sure I will. And your problems will continue. 'Cause they started when I wasn't around."

"Let me tell you about problems," he said.

I leaned forward so our heads nearly met over the desk, ready to hear the worst, when we were interrupted by a knock on the door. Sid put a finger to his lips, and I nodded. "Come in," he said.

The door opened, and a woman who looked vaguely familiar stepped in, followed by two other men I'd never seen before. The last person in the somber line was Lynnette.

Lynnette was tall, lanky, her head hovered above even the guys who stood in front of her. Her kinky blond permed hair, when not tied back, flowed to her shoulders. Today, however, she wore it in a smooth french roll, which made her appear more professional than usual. She and Sid cleared off four chairs, and she invited the others to sit down. As she sat down herself, moving the tails of her red jacket to keep them from wrinkling, she noticed me.

"What's she doing here?"

"Hello, yourself, Lynnette," I said.

"Sid?"

"I hired her to help out with our troubles. D'Arcy, this is Susan Jenkins, the health inspector for the Dearborn area."

"Nice to meet you." I remembered suddenly that she was the woman I'd seen in the car the morning of my hangover. One of the other guys, who looked a bit like a mafia bodyguard with slicked back black hair, was the guy who'd been sitting next to her that day.

"And Martin Carruthers, Jay Little, on the health investigation team. They're looking into the food poisoning death we had last week."

I shook everyone's hands.

"Sid."

"What, Lynnette."

"What is d'Arcy Carter doing here?" She smiled, the crinkling around her face not matching the anger in her eyes.

"D'Arcy quit the deli to become a private investigator. I hired her last week to investigate our food loss problems. She has reason to believe the food loss is tied in with our health problems."

"What food loss?" Susan Jenkins asked.

Lynnette's face contorted for an instant, but then she clamped her lips, biting them together with her teeth. Her nostrils flared.

I answered. "For the last month or so, the food loss rate has gone up by almost one hundred per cent. Sid wanted to know why, so he hired me. If I can be of any help to you in your investigation, Susan, please let me know."

"Well, I appreciate that. I must admit, I never expected this kind of trouble at Nouveau Deli. I'm at a loss. This restaurant has never been any problem for me. Always the highest marks on its health inspections. I'm talking 98, 95, then 99 just last year."

She ran her fingers through her short brown hair. I thought she looked nervous. Maybe she was. She'd been the health inspector the last time through. She might think her job was also on the line. Or maybe she was the one accepting payola from Lynnette, as Joe Canelli implied. I tried to imagine a lover relationship between her and Lynnette. Stranger things have happened, but I couldn't see Lynnette as a lesbian—Oops, I wasn't listening.

"I thought maybe I'd find the employees had let things slide since the last inspection," she said, "But I have found nothing to make me believe this is the case."

"Ma'am, I think it's a case of sabotage."

"Excuse me?"

I watched Lynnette's face for a reaction. It was like a stone, indicating nothing, her eyes glued on Sid's. "Someone is purposely leaving salads out of refrigeration to warm up into the danger zone."

The woman's mouth opened, closed, then opened again. "Why on earth would someone be doing that?"

"I'm not sure. I plan to find out."

Susan straightened her back and narrowed her eyes. "We will cooperate with you if you cooperate with us. But realize this, we have begun a full investigation into the problem. You will not be immune from this investigation."

CHAPTER 25
"Building up the Case"

Once the health department had left, I was alone with Sid and Lynnette, who had not stopped glaring at each other. "What the hell do you think you're doing, Sid? Hiring an alleged private detective? Nouveau Angela Lansbury is more like it."

"I have reason to believe we're being sabotaged."

"I have reason to believe you're an asshole."

"Now, Lynnette—"

"Don't 'now' me."

"Lynnette," I said, "I'd like to ask you some questions, too."

"Fuck off." She didn't even bother to take her eyes from Sid to look at me. Instead, she glared a moment longer, then whirled on her heels and left the room, slamming the door behind her.

"Trouble at home?" I asked.

"You've got to clear this up fast," he said. "Right away."

"Understood." I got up to leave.

"And, d'Arcy."

"Yeah?"

"Lay off Lynnette, okay?"

"Are you sure it's not her?"

He didn't answer. He propped his head on a fist, then passed his other hand over his eyes.

"I take that to mean you can't be sure," I said. "Then I can't lay off her, can I?"

"I know it's not her."

"How?"

Then it dawned on me. "Oh, because she wouldn't have killed Ben Mitchell, right?"

His shoulders slumped.

"She was having an affair with him, wasn't she?"

Sid didn't answer.

"Sid, what did Ben do for a living?"

He cleared his throat. "He, uh, he worked for the government."

"I know that much. What did he do for the government?"

He looked up at me, surprised by the harshness of my words. "He, uh, scheduled inspections of various types."

"Including health."

"Yes."

"Did Lynnette ever manipulate when we would be investigated?"

He shrugged his shoulders. "I don't know. I don't think so. Not with my knowledge."

"Then I still can't lay off her, can I?"

I left before he had a chance to answer me.

No further along, I thought. I locked my bike to a sign and walked into the gym. Shoulder and leg day. I did some abs, too. It was actually a great workout, the first one in well over a week. I sweated through forty five minutes of a shoulder work, then did seven sets of squats.

Squats suck. To quote a male bodybuilder I've since forgotten the name of, "I've done thousands of squats in my life, and I've hated every one." I don't think squats get easier, either. Ever. I'm always out of breath after doing a set of fifteen, but I rest and go on to another.

An hour and a half later, I was starved. I grabbed a carbo-hydrate drink to replenish some energy. I drank it slowly as I pedalled home.

I turned the corner on Farnum, and nearly ran into my two biker buddies, Randy and Chet. "Oh, sorry, guys."

"In a rush?"

"Sort of." I looked at my watch. It was 5:30. "I'm supposed to go to a barbecue tonight."

"This will just take a minute."

"Excuse me?"

"Bronco has a message for you."

"Bronco. You mean, Jennifer's Bronco?" For some reason, I'd never connected these two parts of my life together before.

Randy nodded. "He's inside."

"Well—"

"It's okay," Chet said. "We won't hurt you."

Against my better judgment, I followed the two of them inside, carrying my bike along with me. In the living room, the furniture was all black leather or leather-look. Bronco sat in the middle of a big couch, two women who weren't Jennifer on either side of him. For some reason, it pissed me off to see him two-timing her. Okay, three-timing was more like it.

He was smoking a bong when I walked in. He put it down when he saw me, and indicated the chair next to the couch.

"So, you're a member of this—uh—motorcycle group, would you call it?"

"Gang." Bronco shrugged his shoulders and smiled slowly in answer. He picked up a beer bottle and swigged from it. "My message is from Jennifer."

"Why doesn't she talk to me?"

"She wants you to lay off with your questions at the deli."

This was the second time today someone'd asked me to

lay off a portion of the case. "Why?"

"There are things you don't know, maybe don't want to understand—"

"Look, I got a message for Jennifer. You tell her to call me and talk to me. Not through you. There are things I need to know."

"She said to lay off."

"And I'm telling her I can't." I stood up. "Look, someone died on my shift. Do you know how that makes me feel? It's too important a thing to lay off of, as you call it. I feel responsible, and I've got to get to the bottom of it."

Total silence followed my announcement. Out of the corner of my eye, I thought I saw Randy nodding his head.

Bronco took another swig of beer. "Yeah, well, I gave you the message."

"You did. Let her know what I told you."

"Sure."

I turned to leave. As I did so, I noticed the entire wall by the door was stacked from the floor almost to the ceiling with wrapped boxes. "Chet, I heard it was your birthday, but you've gotten a ton of presents," I said lightly.

Chet laughed as he opened the door for me. "Those aren't mine. Every time we have a birthday, everybody buys one present for the birthday boy, and one for a Toys for Tots kind of thing. Then we give them out at Christmas. The Harley Santas."

Harley Santas. God, what would they come up with next? I waved as I got on my bike, then pedalled off. Glad I hadn't been killed. I realized I didn't mind Chet or Randy. They seemed like nice enough guys. And I thought what a neat idea they had to help needy kids.

But, boy was I pissed at Bronco and Jennifer. What kind of shit message was that? She had to know something, something she desperately wanted to keep covered up.

Peyton was sweating and drinking glass after glass of water when I came in. "You gotta see the kind of progress I made."

He led the way upstairs to the attic. The whole place looked like it had been bombed out. Peyton had demolished the back wall, leaving not a shred of panelling. The attic extended out four feet past where the wall had been, so the ceiling slanted down to meet the floor.

Meanwhile, he'd pulled up the plywood from the floor to expose the rafters. Remnants of the debris were stacked in piles around the attic floor, laying where he hadn't pulled it up.

"See, I've double-joisted a couple areas, here," he pointed to the far left corner. Where he pointed, I could see there were twice as many rafter 2x4's as there were elsewhere in the attic. "And here. For the bathtub and the bed. Give it extra strength."

"You did this so soon?"

"Well, I had some help from a couple classmates."

"God, at this rate, it'll all be done in less than a month."

"This was the easy part. From here out, the work's gonna be hard. I'll have to barter with some roofers to get some help."

I nodded. "Have I told you before, Peyton, that you're incredible? This is great."

"Yep. So, let's celebrate."

"That reminds me." I walked down the stairs and Peyton followed me. I could hear Pantera mewing on the other side of the door.

I opened it, and caught the cat as she tried to skitter up the steps. "Oh, no, you don't. I got an invitation for you and me to go to a barbecue."

"At Tim's."

I sighed. "Oh, Peyton. What am I going to do? It'll never work out."

"What kind of attitude is that? If you don't think it'll work out, trust me, it won't."

"You're one to talk. So many of your relationships have worked out so well."

He rubbed the back of my shoulders. "I speak from experience. It's part of my own problem. I just haven't thought my relationships would work out in the past. That don't mean I stop trying."

I threw my hands up. "But if you have this feeling in your gut, what says it isn't true? Some people do have forebodings that turn out correct, you know."

"Is that what you really think?"

I was surprised, not to mention confused, by his question. Because the fact was, I was getting different signals from my subconscious. Just last night I'd had a dream. Tim and I were dancing. I think it was at St. Andrews Hall again. And a voice I couldn't recognize had said, "This is the man you will marry."

I'd woken up in a cold sweat.

"Peyton, you and I, we get along so well together. I can talk to you about anything, and you've been the greatest housemate I could dream of. But, if we got interested in each other, that would be the end. We wouldn't be able to talk normally to each other again."

"That's not true."

"I get so tongue-tied with him, Peyton."

He laughed and turned me around so he could rub my shoulders right where a pair of knots had sprung up. "Sure, I'll go with you tonight. You're just uptight about it. Forget you're interested in him and just pretend you're talking to me."

"Yeah, right." I closed my eyes, trying to talk myself into having a good time.

CHAPTER 26
"Getting a Grilling"

Peyton and I were ready to go by seven p.m. We hopped into his car, and I gave him the directions Tim had given me on the phone. It was hot. By the time Peyton's air conditioner had cooled things down, my pants and the back of my t-shirt had already stuck to my thighs and the small of my back.

It was a fifteen minute drive to Tim's apartment. Seven and a half miles, roughly a twenty minute bike ride. He lived almost in Dearborn Heights. I'd seriously considered stopping off at the mall as we passed it, rather than going on to the barbecue, but I knew Peyton wouldn't have approved had I even suggested it.

"Fashionably late," he said. He pulled into a parking space and checked his watch.

"Speak for yourself. I have no fashion sense whatsoever."

I picked up the bottle of White Zinfandel I'd chilled in the fridge a few weeks ago but never opened, and we hiked up the walk to Tim's entryway. Peyton buzzed the apartment.

"Come on in, it's open," was the reply over the intercom. I pulled the door and Peyton followed me in. So much for the security system in this place.

Tim had once told me he lived in a squalid apartment that didn't allow cats. I could see what he meant. There was litter in the entryway, enough so that it looked like a garbage can had been upended at the top of the stairs, and wind had swirled it all the way to the bottom. Old banana peels, paper, and other uni-dentifiable rubbish lay in every corner. The smell was over-whelming. Add to this onslaught the fact that the hall hadn't been painted in several years.

We picked our way to the second floor. One of the doors flew open. Standing in front of me was the most gorgeous woman I'd ever seen. That included some of the models I met in my class at Princeton.

She had blunt cut blond hair, tied in a neat braid hanging down to her waist. Her straight white teeth glittered when she smiled. Perfect cupid's bow lips, deep olive colored eyes, and a reed thin body. So Tim must have another girlfriend. And she was a beauty. What had he seen in me?

"Well, come on in, things are just getting started," she said with a trace of Kentucky accent. "My name's Barbra, what's yours?"

"This is Peyton, and I'm d'Arcy."

"D'Arcy, of course, I've heard so much about you," she said, but her eyes were not on me. Instead she smiled wider and gripped Peyton's hand. "So nice to meet you, Peyton. Tim said I'd probably enjoy meeting you." I stepped inside, and left them to chatter in the hall.

In spite of the hallway's appearance, Tim's apartment was small, but attractive. It had recently been repainted in clear white enamel, probably by Tim himself, so that it shone in the evening sunlight. He had a lot of nice art prints which hung on every wall.

On second look, I noticed some of the 'art prints' were actual art pieces. They were fairly unusual, but attractive. One had murky shades of brown and green, which nearly hid a photograph of a beautiful woman. Another was a small box covered in glass. Inside were buttons, a clothespin, and a tiny painting of an ironing board.

"Looking at my mixed media collection?" I looked up and located the voice. Tim was in the small beige kitchenette, dressed in a black apron which read, "Life is hell without Zinfandel." He'd draped a red and white checkered towel around his neck, and he had a tray of raw hamburgers in one hand, a tray of sausages in the other.

"They're very different, aren't they?" I said.

"Couple of my friends are artists. As I get money, I invest in some of their pieces, to help them out. My goal is to make them famous, so the art will be worth more."

I laughed. "I like this one." I pointed to the one near the kitchen, the one with the ironing board. "It reminds me of a dollhouse."

He put the trays down and wiped his hands on the towel. "D'Arcy, thanks for coming." He took me in both arms and kissed me, hard, on the mouth. When I thought he would stop, he didn't. Instead, he started licking at my closed lips, insisting that I open them. The next thing I knew, I was breathless. I needed to come up for air.

"Well," I said, when we finally parted, and we both laughed. Awkwardly, I held out the bottle of wine. "Here. I hope you like it."

"Terrific choice. It's a great picnic wine. I'll open it. Want some?"

I refused, instead asking for water.

"In training?" he asked.

"For what?"

"A bodybuilding contest, maybe."

"No, I just, well, I don't want to get out of control again."

"Oh, that." Tim looked down at the plate, and picked up a handful of raw hamburger, which he patted into a round, flat disk. "Look, I don't know what got into me. But if I said anything, you know—"

"No, it wasn't you. No, I was embarrassed, that's all."

"Oh, d'Arcy, you don't have to be embarrassed. I had a great time, and I hoped you did, too." Still, he wouldn't look at me. "No, I'm afraid maybe I said something, untoward."

"Untoward?"

"Yeah, you know, something I shouldn't have told you. Do you think I did?"

I had no idea what he was talking about. "Nothing I can remember. But then, a lot of what we talked about—" I stopped. I refused to admit to him that I couldn't remember most of the conversation after a certain point that night. "Don't worry about it, Tim, you're fine."

I fell silent, and he didn't say anything more. I wanted another kiss like that last one I'd received. Just thinking about it, I wanted to go with him to find his bedroom, and forget about the other guests.

I followed him like an eager pup as he carried the meat to the gas grill. It was on the small balcony overlooking a particularly dingy swimming pool. "How do you like your burger?" he asked

"Well."

"Really? Me, too. Don't meet too many well done fans in this world."

"True." Okay, enough with the one word answers. Think of something intelligent to say. I sipped at my glass of water. Okay, not intelligent. Just say something. "Anything I can do to help?"

"No, I think we're set. My boss, Brad, should be showing up with his wife. I invited Ralph, your boss, too, with Genevieve, of course."

"You did? Oh, that's right. You know them." I looked over at Peyton, who now sat very close to the blond on the couch. They were in rapt conversation. "So, who's Barbra?" I said in a tone that would not be overheard.

Tim looked over at the two of them, smiling with obvious pleasure. "One of the junior partners at the firm. Pretty, isn't she? We dated a couple times, but it didn't work out. We don't have much in common."

My heart sank. I wasn't really sure Tim and I had much in common, either. What didn't they have in common? I wanted to know, but couldn't get myself to ask. I watched silently as he put four burgers on the grill. "Peyton, how do you like your burgers?" Tim asked.

Peyton's eyes never left Barbra's as he said, "Rare, please."

Tim winked at me. "See what I mean? Barbra's a rare fan, too. Not bad for only having met Peyton once." He licked his finger and sketched a one in the air.

"What?" Then it dawned on me. "Tim, did you set Peyton up?"

"Well, yeah. I thought they might like each other. And if they don't, hey, it's a party, who cares?" He turned two of the burgers over. "Do you think you could grab a beer for me from the fridge? I don't want to screw up the burgers." He chuckled behind my back as I walked away.

I walked to the kitchen area and pulled open the refrigerator door. Inside was a tossed salad, fruit salad, and what looked like potato salad, for the party, I guessed. In addition, there was a half gallon of skim milk, a few eggs, and a variety of veggies in the crispers.

I found the beer, a six pack of a local amber ale in glass bottles, behind a thawing frozen orange juice can. I pulled one out, thought of pulling another for myself, then thought against it.

"You guys want anything to drink?" I asked. Peyton shook his head. Barbra chose not to react at all. I walked over to Tim and gave him his beer. There was a knock at the door, and I gestured to say I'd answer it.

Ralph and Genevieve stood on the threshhold. As soon as she saw me, she opened her purse and pulled out some 4x6 photos. They were of her daughter and the brand new grandbaby. The baby had a light fringe of flax-colored fuzz on her head. I oohed and aahed. "Now, it's a little girl, isn't it?"

"Yes, indeed," Genevieve said. "Ann Marie."

Ralph excused himself silently and went to stand next to Tim. Genevieve shrugged and rolled her eyes. "Men," she seemed to say.

"The sweater set will look adorable. The color will go with her hair," I said. Genevieve beamed.

Ralph said to Tim, "You really ought to get the managers to fix the security system here. That hall's a pigsty."

"I know, I keep trying," Tim began. Too many people were talking for me to hear the rest of that conversation.

Right behind Genevieve and Ralph were two folks I assumed to be Tim's boss and his wife. I introduced myself, offered everyone drinks, and generally played hostess. Tim handed burgers to Peyton and Barbra, and asked the others what they wanted.

The party was pleasant, but I felt like I'd gone to meet his parents, and the parents had found me amazingly stupid. I decided to just be quiet, and say nothing. Maybe that way I wouldn't bore anyone with my conversation.

We finished our burgers, and Tim invited us into the dining room for coffee and brownies. We all crowded around the small table with six chairs. "How should we sit?" Genevieve asked. "Do you have any more chairs?"

Tim shook his head, and scratched his chin. "Hmm."

"That's okay," Peyton said. "Barb, why don't you sit on my lap?"

She giggled, and freely complied. Before anyone could say anything, Tim smiled and said, "D'Arcy, you can sit on mine."

Everyone around the table laughed, and I couldn't control my own nervous laughter. "Oh, Tim, I don't—"

"Go ahead, d'Arcy, don't be shy," Ralph said. "As far as I know, Tim doesn't bite."

Tim sat down, and I perched precariously on one of his knees. He adjusted my hips so I sat squarely on both legs.

Over coffee, Ralph turned the conversation to business. "Got a call from the guy in New York."

"Yeah? Any news?"

"Well, there's no record on him, if that's what you mean. But one interesting thing came up. Seems shortly before he left Brooklyn, his family's deli went up in smoke."

"Hmm. Arson?"

"It was never proved. I don't know if that has any bearing on this case, but keep it in the back of your mind. So, anything new in the deli biz, d'Arcy?"

Sitting on Tim's lap, I was having trouble thinking clearly. "Oh, the, uh, health department's now in on it. Sid's, uh, Sid's screaming at me to clear it up. Fast. But then, she's, I mean, he's, telling me to lay off his, Lynnette." Oh, God, d'Arcy, try to say just one sentence without stumbling over every word. "And Jennifer sent me a message to get off the case."

He laughed. "That's usually a sign that you're getting closer to the real answer. Everyone wants to shut you up."

"Any news on Joe Canelli's past?"

"Oh, yeah, Joe's record is relatively clean. Parking tickets, drunk and disorderlies, that kind of thing. Nothing to make me think he had to run away from New York."

"I'm not real surprised to hear that, I guess. I don't think it's him."

"Is this your new investigator, Ralph?" Brad asked, reaching for the cream. "I didn't realize you'd finally hired someone."

Ralph nodded. "Yes, Tim gave me a glowing report about her work up north, in Grayling."

I blushed to the roots of my heart, I could feel it. So that was why I'd gotten the job so easily. Tim had basically forced Ralph to hire me. I had nothing to do with it. Now I realized I probably wouldn't have gotten the job if it hadn't been for Tim.

I felt humiliated. Never before had I relied on someone to get me a job. My father and I haven't spoken because I refused to use his help to make my way in the world. I hadn't asked for Tim's help, either. Just who did he think he was?

I grant that I haven't done well as a free agent, but at least the only person I could blame was myself.

Did Tim think I was so desperate that I needed his help to get into the one field I thought I had a chance of succeeding at? And here, I'd thought I'd done this one on my own. I stood on the edge of a deep hole, and I could feel a tugging to jump inside it.

It took me several minutes before I could think of what to say. I turned back to the case, to save face. I didn't look at Tim; I forced myself to be coherent. "I think she knows something."

"Who?" Ralph replied. "Lynnette, or Jennifer?"

"Jennifer. Well, Lynnette may, too, but I think Jennifer saw someone messing around in the refrigerator case shortly before Cille got sick."

"This is pleasant dinner conversation," Barbra said. "Let's change the subject. Seen any good movies lately?"

I wanted to leave soon after that conversation, but Peyton ignored me until nearly midnight. I remained silent the rest of the evening. Then, bluntly, I said, "Tim, I've got to get to the deli early tomorrow."

Peyton looked at me in surprise. "I thought—" But then, he must have noticed the look on my face, because he said, "Yeah, she gets up at 5:30 to work at that stupid place."

A chorus of sympathetic voices greeted this announcement. Tim walked me to the door. He tried to kiss me, but I turned my face toward Peyton, and his lips brushed my hair.

He grabbed my hand as I tried to leave, forcing me to look back at him. I wanted to hit him.

"Call me," he said.

I nodded numbly, and left.

When Peyton and I finally got to our car, he was talking a mile a minute. "Wasn't she gorgeous? And, God, we have so much in common. Can you believe, her hobby is carpentry? Finish carpentry. She may come over tomorrow to help out with upstairs—"

"So, can I take it that you like her, Peyton?" I realized I'd said it through clenched teeth, and I willed my jaw to relax.

"Well, yeah, sure. Didn't you?"

"I can't say I really talked to her at all. Someone was monopolizing her time, I'd say."

"Oh. Sorry." He looked at me for a moment, until he recognized the expression on my face. "Didn't it go well with you and Tim?"

"Strained," I said. "What a fucking asshole."

"D'Arcy, why do you say that?"

I didn't mean to voice my fears, they just came rushing out. "Oh, Peyton, he got the job for me, practically forced poor Ralph to take me on. And now, now I feel even more in need of proving myself, and what if I fail? What if I never figure out who's behind this case? Oh, God, I could kill him."

"Oh." Peyton tried to be quiet. He drummed his fingers along the top of the steering wheel. It was a mannerism that reminded me of Tim, and I felt my stomach as it tried to become my heart. Then Peyton played with the gear shift, rubbing his hands up and down as though it were a phallic symbol. The next thing I knew, he was off again, speaking at top speed, the southern accent thick.

My stomach remained where my heart had been, my heart sinking to fill the void. So now, I was going to lose Peyton, too, to a lovely blond woman named Barbra.

I tuned him out, turning to my own gloomy thoughts.

When we turned left on Paisley, the first thing I saw was the cop car. The lights were out, but I could see their reflection back from Peyton's headlights. The engine was off. Two policemen sat in the front seat.

Peyton slowed his car to a crawl. "What do you think they're here for? I didn't do anything." Peyton said.

I patted his hand and shrugged my shoulders. "I think they're here for me, Peyton, not you. But we're about to find out."

Peyton parked the car in the driveway, and we walked to the door. Peyton tried to ignore the shadows of the men as they opened the police car doors and walked across our lawn. "It's because I'm a black man, I just know it."

"Stop it, Peyton. I told you, they're here for me."

"You? Why?"

"Ssh." When I stopped to unlock the door, I turned to find the cops right behind us.

"D'Arcy W. Carter?" The woman said.

"Yes."

"We'd like to ask you a few questions," she said. "I understand you were supervisor the day Charlie Foster was killed. Is that true?"

CHAPTER 27
"Watched Like a Hawk"

I had been wondering what took them so long to track me down. I led the two policemen in and pointed to the couch. They sat down together at almost the same instant, reminding me of old FBI movies. "Yes, I was the supervisor," I said. I sat opposite them in the overstuffed chair. Peyton slipped away, as though hiding from the law.

"Why don't you tell us what happened that day?"

"First, I have to say you have me at a distinct disadvantage. You know my name, but I do not know yours."

"I'm Lieutenant Tyler, this is Sergeant Canfield. I believe you've met him," the woman said.

I nodded at Lieutenant Tyler, then the sergeant. "I didn't recognize you at first. Welcome back to my house, Sergeant Canfield. What are you doing here?"

He bowed slightly. "I told the lieutenant about you, and she thought I might put you more at ease, since you already knew me."

I nodded. "Well, I got there at six o'clock, and started setting up the case. Cecille Brown arrived next, after I'd finished the salad refrigerator, then came Jennifer Case. I finished putting desserts in the dessert case, and then—"

"Skip the minutiae, Miss Carter. Who was there?" Tyler said.

"Me, Cille Edwards, Jennifer Case, Charlie Foster, the people on the sandwich line. I don't remember who was making sandwiches, other than Muller. Sid came in later."

"Charles Foster died by choking on his own vomit, but his illness was brought on by food poisoning. Do you have any idea where he may have contracted the salmonella?"

"As far as I could tell, it was ham and cheese potato salad. So it was definitely salmonella?"

"Did I say that?"

Sergeant Canfield looked at her and laughed. "Yes, you did."

Lieutenant Tyler looked at him, then back at me. "Ham and potato salad. Is that a surmization on your part, or did you plant it?"

I thought it best not to point out that 'surmization' was not a word. "Sergeant—"

"I'm a lieutenant."

"I'm sorry. Lieutenant, I am not a murderer. In fact, I was hired by Sid Field, the owner of Nouveau Deli, to investigate a problem that had developed."

"Hired?"

"I'm an apprenticed private investigator. I used to work at Nouveau Deli. Since I'd been trained as a supervisor at Nouveau Deli, Sid thought I could help him out."

"You're a private investigator, then?"

I nodded.

"What firm?"

"Hughes Investigations."

"Let me see your license."

My eyes sketched the zebra pattern of the area rug. "I don't have one."

"You mean you're practicing without a license?"

"No. I mean I am training to be an investigator. I was just hired by Ralph Hughes, and I don't even have a set of cards yet."

The lieutenant cleared her throat. I wondered if she had any idea what to do with me. She certainly didn't believe me. "I know Hughes. So how did you get involved with Nouveau Deli?"

"I told you. I used to work at Nouveau Deli. Sid thought I'd be able to go undercover better than most untrained individuals. Untrained at the deli, that is. I think he also hoped I'd be cheaper than most P.I.'s."

"I see. What were you investigating?"

"Well, ma'am, according to Sid, they had developed a serious food loss problem. In the last few days, I became convinced the food loss situation and the food poisoning deaths were linked."

"Deaths?"

Oh, God, it had just slipped out. Now what was I supposed to say? "Death, I mean death. Only one. But, uh, we've had a few other employees contract food poisoning."

"You said deaths."

"Look, I've never been questioned by the police before. I just mis-spoke."

The lieutenant snapped her notebook closed with one hand. "Do you plan to cooperate with the police on this case or not?"

"Of course. I told you that. Why wouldn't I?"

"See that you do. Have a good night, Miss Carter." The two police left my house, but not before Sergeant Canfield turned and winked at me.

Saturday was the day I personally dreaded, because I had a ten hour shift on the line. No matter what kind of shape I was in, ten hour shifts drained the hell out of me. I don't know what Sid could have been thinking, because I couldn't work on this case and also have these hours. He should never have let Jennifer schedule me this way.

I woke up at 9:30, already feeling drained. The first decision I made was to bag weight training today, not because I didn't want to do my arms and calves, but because I didn't have the energy nor did I have the time.

Quickly I dressed and ate some cereal, and downed some coffee, too. Then I got ready for the long bike ride there.

It was hot as Hades outside, too. I slathered on some sun block and wore a baseball cap and sunglasses, but it didn't help much. The construction area near my house had gotten worse. I stopped for a minute to wipe off some sweat, and I watched the air come off in waves on the hot, broken concrete.

At least I wasn't a construction worker today. Thank God I gave up that job after only a few months. I didn't have to bake in the sun all day. Only part of it. I pedalled down Middle Belt Road. I'd probably have to work a couple hours outside cleaning up the empty paper plates off a scattering of picnic tables. The rest of the time, I would work inside in the alleged air-conditioning.

The ride seemed longer than usual. It was probably the heat, sucking it all out of me. I parked and locked my bike, and went inside the back way.

For once, the deli was bustling again, after a week of near inactivity. In the crowd, I noticed the health inspector and her two boys, whose names I couldn't remember, out from the health department. They were watching everyone closely, trying to make sure all the refrigerators were set at under forty two degrees, all the heaters were 140 degrees or more.

In spite of our evaluators, Jennifer's shift ran smoother than an ice covered lake. She actually gave me a smile when I walked in, the first one in several days. "You're pick-up for the first leg of your shift," she said. I made an okay sign and went back to the office to get my cash drawer.

Sid was there, waiting for me. "Anything new?" he said as I tried to count my drawer.

I finished the quarters and wrote the total down. "No, Sid, and I won't have time today to learn much."

"Why not? I'm paying you good money to—"

"Look, you're the one who let Jennifer give me nine and ten hour days. If you'd really cared about me doing this fast, I would've been scheduled only three days on the line. You can't have your cake and eat it, too, damn it."

Sid remained silent as I counted dimes and nickels. As I started on the pennies, he said, "Well, you're on only three days next week."

"Then, maybe I can solve the case next week. God knows, I want to get out of here, probably faster than you want me to."

"Is working here really that bad?"

I dropped the pennies in the drawer. "Sid, eight, ten, sometimes twelve hours, on our feet the whole time. Thankless customers who yell at us any chance they get. Understaffed all the time. Back aching, legs aching, and rotten choice in food. The best rate I'll ever see is $6.75 an hour. Oh, I forget, I'm a woman, my rates are lower than the men who work here. But still, you make squat, unless you're allowed in the hallowed halls of management, but you've got to suck management's feet to get there. Then you make fifty grand or more a year."

Sid squirmed a little, which made me think he made much more. "Level with me, Sid. How much did Ned get to become kitchen manager?"

He mumbled something.

"What?"

"Started at fifty."

"Fifty. And the people who really do the work are making ten. It's sinful, Sid. You wonder why you can't keep good help. And while I'm at it, how come every woman who works here makes less than every man who works here? That's sexual discrimination, Sid. Your natives are restless here, and then you have the gall to wonder what's created the food poisoning problem."

"Ssh," he said, a look of pure fear pouring out of his eyes.

"Treat the peons right, and maybe you won't have the problems you're seeing now." I walked out of the office, not bothering to finish counting the drawer. What did I care whether it was off or not? As soon as this case was settled, I was outta here. I just wished I could settle it.

At two, I got a break, and I downed a Reuben, no russian, trying to make myself feel better. Now that I'd had time to think about it, I'd realized I shouldn't have blown up at Sid. It wasn't really all his fault what had happened at Nouveau Deli. Lynnette had had a hand in it, too.

The fatty corned beef and swiss didn't help. I just ended up feeling sluggish and even angrier. The sauerkraut was giving me heartburn. After my break, I was put on the floor, where I refilled ice, made sure the pop machines were filled, made coffee, swept the floor, and picked up after people.

The customers were slobbier than usual. They left torn napkins in shreds to flutter all over the small patio in the wind. Mustard had been squirted in op-art patterns on one of the indoor tables. They ordered much more than they could ever eat, and then left it, piled on top of other food, so I had to sort it all out and save any glass plates for the dishwasher, ditching the rest.

One thing I learned in my years of food service was to pick up after myself and eat neatly when I was in a restaurant. No one wanted to clean up my trash, and I didn't like cleaning other people's.

Of all the jobs at the deli, floor work was the most thankless one. Once you were sent out there, supervisors and managers both forgot you existed. The heat was baking me alive outside, but I was the only one trying to take care of trash cans and customers and ice and pops and coffee.

And everywhere I went, a health department official trotted after me. When I went to the ice machine, they made sure I turned my scoop the right way, so nothing could fall into it from the sky. I man-handled a carbon dioxide tank while they watched, not one of them offering to help with the fifty pound cylinder.

Did I make the coffee right? Was I keeping everything clean enough? Did I change my bleach bucket every two hours?

All the while, I seethed inside, and I refused to allow myself time to think about why I was so angry. It wasn't just life at the deli, and I knew it.

I finally turned to one of them and said, "Would you lay off already?"

"What are you worried about? You're doing a good job."

"Then get off my back. I'm tired of being shadowed by you goons."

He shot me a suspicious look, as though as soon as he turned his back, I'd poison the decaf. But he finally walked away.

CHAPTER 28
"Father Confessor"

9:00 didn't come soon enough. By the time I clocked out, I wanted to use the time clock as a punching bag. But unfortunately, I wasn't finished yet.

Lynnette was in the owners' office, alone. When she looked up and saw me, her eyes narrowed. "What do you want?"

"I want to know why you want to sell this place."

"I'm tired of it. I've been watching you. You hate this place as much as I do. Surely you can understand why."

"No, I can't really understand it. You make a fortune at this place."

"Not as much as you might think."

"Managers make at least fifty grand. I think that means you're making even more."

"So what does that have to do with you?"

I was being too pushy. I knew it. I was putting her on edge, and she wouldn't answer any questions at this rate. I sat on top of her desk and forced myself to take a deep breath.

Then I said, "Who do you want to sell this place to?"

"That's no business of yours."

"Look, people are getting killed. I'm here to tell you Nouveau Deli is being sabotaged. Sid was right. And he hired me to find out who, so it is my business. Just tell me this one thing."

Lynnette doodled a bunch of circles on the blotter of her desk. The wedding ring she used to wear was gone.

"Joe Canelli," she finally said.

"Joe Canelli." I stood up again. "You're joking."

"I'm not. He's interested and he's willing to pay a lot of money."

"Do you know what happened to his New York deli?"

Lynnette looked up at me in surprise. "How do you know what happened to him in New York?"

"Hughes Investigations ran a background check on him. How do you know what happened to him in New York?"

She ran her fingers through her hair, messing up what was left of the left hand part. "It wasn't arson, if that's what you think."

"I know it couldn't be proved."

"It wasn't arson," she said, flatly. She stood up and gestured to the door with her finger. "Joe's wife is my cousin. She would not marry an arsonist. Besides, why burn a building that wasn't insured?"

"Joe didn't have insurance?"

"No. See, he's not what you think he is."

Since I'd finally gotten her talking, I tried one more question. "So these health department people that are hanging around. Which one did you pay off?" Before it was out of my mouth, I knew I'd said it wrong.

"What?"

I was silent.

"Who on earth told you I was doing that?"

"Joe Canelli."

Her hands clenched in fists on either side of her. "I would never do such a thing. How can you have worked here for a year and not known how important sanitation is to me? Now, just go."

It was true. She was furious with me, she was turning me out of her office, but I had to believe her answer. I turned to go, but turned back. "You and Sid having troubles?"

I didn't expect her to even deign to answer me, but I must have distracted her. She looked at her ring finger as though reading my mind. "I've filed for divorce, yes."

"I'm sorry to hear about that." I turned again, reaching for the door.

"D'Arcy."

"Yeah."

"There are some things all the money this deli could make can't buy. It took me six years to discover that."

So that's why Sid wanted me to check out old Joe. Maybe Joe was sabotaging the food to force the sale in his favor. The price was bound to go down on a deli with health violation problems. But why didn't Joe mention he wanted Nouveau Deli, instead of bad-mouthing it like he did? He seemed like the type who'd gloat in front of the media about the pending sale.

I guessed it was time to put Joe Canelli back on the investigation list.

It was only slightly cooler riding back home after night fall. A breeze had picked up, but it was a hot breeze, filled with the stagnant smells of drying tar, fallen ice cream cones, and other signs of a hot summer.

I really needed to talk to someone, anyone. I was tired and depressed and needed someone who'd just listen without speaking. This was why I loved living with Peyton. He was the perfect confidante.

I nearly cried after I got home and found out Peyton wasn't there. He'd left a note, however. "Went out with Barbra. Don't wait up. Ha ha."

I found Pantera and hugged her tightly to my breast, but her purring made me even sadder. It had been a bad day, destined to get worse if I didn't do something about it.

No idea why I did it, but after I'd walked around the house three or four times, Pantera clinging to my shoulder, I stopped at the phone nook. I picked up the phone and dialed a number from memory.

It wasn't until someone picked up on the other end that I realized whom I'd called. Why on earth had I called here, except possibly to get beaten down even farther? I almost hung up. Instead, I gulped down some pride and said, "Hello, Father?"

"Is that you, d'Arcy? What's wrong?"

"Why do you think something is wrong?"

"Why else would you call?"

Why else, indeed? Pantera leapt to the ground, probably disgusted with me. "I don't run to you with my problems, normally."

He was silent. So long, I thought he'd hung up. Then he said, "That's true, you don't. You sound sad."

The sound of his concern almost made me cry. "Yeah, well, rough week. I've gotten myself a job. Mom should be pleased to hear that."

"What is it this time?"

"Father—"

"I'm sorry, I didn't mean anything by that."

"Private investigator?" Go ahead, tell me it's another job I'll fail at. I knew that already.

"What?"

"I am apprenticing to be a private investigator. You know, a detective?"

He cleared his throat. "Well, now, I didn't expect that change of careers. What brought this on?"

"Well, I went up to Grayling a few weeks ago, and—"

"Oh, that's right. You put my doctor in jail."

I knew I should've hung up as soon as I realized whom I'd called. "I'm sorry—"

"No, that's okay, he deserved it. D'Arcy, I—"

"Well, anyway, what I did up there got me thinking. And I'm interested in the investigating field now."

"I'm proud of you. Maybe it's not what I'd want my daughter to do, but if you can be good at it, then go for it."

My mouth dropped open. I couldn't figure out how to close it.

I sat down on the chair next to the phone nook, barely scratching Pantera's head. She mewed again, asking me to get off the phone. "You are?"

"Yes, I am. You did a good job in Grayling, even if Morgan's parents will never speak to us again."

"You think too much about what people in your circle think."

"Now, d'Arcy—"

"Well, thanks." It was the smallest voice I'd heard come out of my mouth in a long time. We were silent. Minutes, hours, I don't know how long. Finally, I said, "Uh, anyway, how's Mother?"

"Fine, fine. She's at David and Marie's. You're about to become an aunt again. Marie went into labor about three hours ago."

I grabbed a pen and wrote a note to myself. I'd be joining Genevieve in the knitting circle if I wanted to get a baby present ready soon. "She did?"

"Yeah. D'Arcy?"

"Yes, Father?"

"Don't be such a stranger. Mother and I miss you."

Out of my mind went all the times they'd yelled at me, telling me I was a good for nothing, a failure at life, an idiot who didn't deserve to go to Cranbrook-Kingswood, and especially not to Princeton.

Out went the years of isolation, all the gifts he gave me that I never wanted, that were too expensive, that were meant to buy my love or my brothers'.

Out went memories of the last conversation I'd had with Mother, when she'd slammed the phone in my ear after I told her I'd quit the job at Nouveau Deli.

Out went the last time I'd talked to my father, three years ago, when he told me if I couldn't learn to be a Carter, then don't bother calling him again. Instead, I heard only what he'd said tonight. He was proud of me, for once in my life.

"I miss you, too, Dad."

When we got off the phone, I curled up into a little ball on the floor under the phone, and I cried.

CHAPTER 29
"Turning a Stone Over Again"

Sunday morning, after a tough arm and calf workout lasting two hours, I showered and changed into jeans and a sweatshirt. During the night, a thunderstorm had come through, leaving the air fresh smelling and cool. It was a welcome relief from the ninety degree weather of the day before.

I rode down to Joe's Cafe, trying to plan my attack. He knew me as a reporter, so I'd have to continue that ruse unless I wanted to blow my cover.

When I walked into the restaurant, I wasn't very surprised to see a line sweeping back and forth in a zigzag pattern which filled the waiting area. The tables were filled; most people were getting their food wrapped to go.

Piss poor prior planning on my part. Sunday brunch crowd. I stepped into line, prepared to wait the fifteen to twenty minutes before I got to the front and stated my business.

A bagel and cream cheese would taste good, I thought, taking one step, then another, to the first bend in the line. My eyes drooped. I suddenly realized how tired I was. I forced myself to stand on one leg, then the other. Practicing my balance helped keep me awake.

"Sesame bagel with lite cream cheese, American Spoon Fruits on the side, I said when I finally made it to the front of the line.

"Out of sesame."

"What do you have?"

"Got garlic, onion, salt."

"Onion, then, but forget the spoon fruit."

"Don't got no spoon fruits anyways. Toasted or not?"

"Toasted. And a cup of coffee. Is Joe in?"

"In the back." The waitress snapped my copy from the order pad and passed it over to me, hanging hers in front of the sandwich maker.

"I'd like to speak to him. Dee Carter."

"Yeah, right, I'll call, but don't expect miracles." She yelled over the phone intercom, then went back to taking orders, leaving me to fend for myself. She'd forgotten to ring me up for my bagel order.

Through the crowd of people, I spotted Joe Canelli moving toward me a few minutes later. He recognized me. Shouted over the din, "Want a drink or something?"

"Coffee?"

He motioned for me to grab a cup from the self-serve island, then to head up to his office, in a series of semaphor-like charades. I poured myself a cup and grabbed two creams. Someone called my name and tossed a bagel my way. Then I excused and pardoned myself like Bugs Bunny in the movie theater, and made my way to his back room. Joe Canelli was my carrot.

His office was tiny in comparison with the offices of Nouveau Deli. Along his walls were floor to ceiling bookshelves stacked with food books, product brochures, samples and accounting ledgers. His desk stood in the center of the room, with walkways hardly a foot wide on all corners. His desk chair was a glorified school chair he'd probably picked up at a garage sale somewhere. It had the writing surface still attached.

Joe motioned for me to sit. I finally selected a pile of picture books and notebooks which was the only place wide enough for a butt to sit on. I sat gingerly, and the pile only made a slight heave, warning me to have my quadriceps ready in case sitting turned into squatting.

In this uncomfortable position, I opened my notebook and looked at Joe Canelli, ready to write.

We sat for some minutes this way. Joe looked back from his desk chair, his eyes registering some curiosity that I'd come back.

I cleared my voice. "So, when I was here last, why didn't you mention you had made an offer on Nouveau Deli?"

"You didn't ask."

"That seems like a bit of a news scoop, you ask me. I would have been interested."

"I'd say you hadn't done your homework."

I looked down at my notebook, trying to think of a come-back for that one. "Well, as a newspaper reporter, we don't have access to—"

"Look," he said, standing up, jabbing his finger into a notebook on his desk, "Who's fooling who, here? I talked with Lynnette—I know Sid's sicced a P.I. on her. My guess is, you're that P.I."

"So what if I am?"

"Look, girlie, I'm not spilling any more information, even if you are a news reporter. What I will tell you is, I have nothing to do with the internal crap going down at Nouveau Deli, and neither does Lynnette. That includes the food poisonings, and Charlie Foster's death."

I stood up, just as the pile I was sitting on collapsed on the floor around my feet. "Why should I believe you? Seems to me, it would be a stroke of luck for you. The price of Nouveau

Deli would go down if word leaks out; you could have the place for a song."

His breath came in a ragged burst. "Choose what you want to believe. But what you say right there is why Lynnette wouldn't do it. I'm buying her out, too, remember."

"Okay, so, she's in the clear. But what about you? Both halves of the negotiation are suddenly cheap for you. You come in, put a big sign up, 'Under New Management,' you're doing good. Or maybe you'd just burn it down and get money from your insurance company. Why wouldn't you do it?"

His face was turning red and purple and white by turns, the blood veins in his temple popping out. I went into a stance, prepared to run if he should pick up something to throw. "Because I don't work that way. I've gotten where I am fair and square."

I looked around the room. "Maybe it's not in your best interests to spread food poisoning rumors. Your own place is a pig sty."

"You bitch!" he yelled as he scooted around his desk, lunging for me.

I was too quick for him. The narrow passages around his desk slowed him down just enough for me to scoot out his office door and down the stairs to the back exit. I could hear him lumbering after me, shouting obscenities and cursing my mother and father. No doubt, if he'd caught me, I'd have been fighting for my breath by now.

I wasted no time hopping on my bike and racing down the street away from Joe's Cafe. It took a few miles for my stomach to remind me I'd left a perfectly good uneaten bagel and coffee in Joe Canelli's office. "Damn it, d'Arcy."

So what had I proven by having pissed off Joe Canelli? Nothing. Sometimes, I was not smart, in spite of being a Princeton graduate. Maybe because I was a Princeton graduate. To punish myself, I rode home at a thirty mile an hour pace, not stopping to catch my breath.

When I reached the construction on Middle Belt Road, my chest burned with the aerobic intake. Sweat was getting into my eyes, running in streaks down my scalp and continuing to where my braid lay, stamped against my back. My calves cried in agony, having been beaten to a pulp once during my workout and another time riding home.

I had to get a car.

CHAPTER 30
"A Puzzle Piece Fits"

I slowed up some as I took the turn down Smith and passed the motorcycle gang's house. No Harleys were parked in the front yard, which was unusual. I wondered what they did besides hang out, drink beer, smoke pot, and buy presents for themselves and their own Toys for Tots program. Did they have jobs? Well, I knew Bronco was a truck driver.

The house felt cool as I entered and left the sunshine on the porch. Upstairs was quiet. Peyton was not around; had he spent the night with Barbra and still not come back? Well, well, well, that's not like him. She must be damn hot.

Pantera sat on the ledge above the radiator. As I came in, she stood on all four legs and stretched her back, then sat on her back haunches and stared at me blankly, as if to say, who the hell are you?

Taking her cue, I stretched my hamstrings and back, added a calf stretch or two, and then went to get a glass of water. While I was at it, I pulled out a can of tuna and ate it, standing up, in the kitchen.

My kitchen was really drab. It hadn't been redone since the forties. It had dark brown cabinets. A hideous, dingy old tile that might once have been beige covered the floor. I wondered if I could convince Peyton to change the colors to white with red, yellow, and blue. Somehow, after two years, he'd never touched the room. I sort of had to wonder why. Maybe kitchens weren't his thing.

I finished the can of tuna, rinsed it out so Pantera wouldn't try to track it down, and threw it away under the sink.

I thought about taking a nap, but most of me didn't want to. What did I want to do? I was at an impasse on this case, getting nowhere fast. Instead of narrowing down my list of suspects, I was making the list bigger.

I realized I should have checked my messages. I went into the hall and found the light blinking three times.

The first message was from Tim, who called to say, "I called just to see how you are."

Fine, thanks.

The second was from Peyton. "Hey, don't worry about me. I met up with Barbra, you know, the girl I met at your Tim's place. We're gonna spend the day together. Forgot to leave you a note. Love ya babe."

The last was Genevieve. "Hi, honey. Why don't you come on over for a picnic? Ralph's got grilling plans, and plenty of meat. My daughter and son-in-law are here. Give me a call and I'll give you directions."

I picked up the phone immediately and dialed the number she'd left. If there was one thing I was learning to count on, it was the fact that talking to Ralph sometimes helped me sort things out. Maybe he could help me this time.

Genevieve gave me the directions. The Hugheses lived in Inkster, about five miles from my house down Ecorse Road. I ran a comb through my hair, changed into shorts and a t-shirt, grabbed my helmet and hit the road.

Fifteen minutes later, I pulled into their driveway. The Hughes family owned a small suburban style house with a one car garage, painted chartreuse with white trim. I tied my bike to the lamp post and hobbled up the walk. My calves had begun to freeze on me, not that I blamed them. I rang the doorbell.

Two seconds, and the door opened. A woman about my age stood in front of me, her blond hair mussed. Her body was slightly saggy in the abdomen, the look of a woman who'd very recently given birth.

"Hi, my name's d'Arcy."

"I'm Charlotte." She opened the door to let me in. "Mom's talked of no one else except you since about a week ago."

"I'm flattered. But that's not true. She's thrilled about you and the baby. That's all I hear about."

Charlotte blushed. "I'm glad." She looked me up and down, though not rudely. "You must work out a lot. You've got great legs."

"Thank you. They're killing me right now. My calves are tight from my workout."

"You ever want a workout partner, let me know. I need to do something about my tummy."

"I work out about six days a week. Just let me know when you want to come along."

"How 'bout tomorrow?" she said, then laughed. "Come on back." She led me past the country styled beige and blue living room, into the avocado green kitchen. There, Genevieve played with the tiny baby I'd heard so much about. The half-finished sweater she'd been making lay on the table in front of the baby's little chair.

"D'Arcy, hello. You've met Charlotte? And this is little Ann Marie."

I cooed over the baby for a moment, then asked Genevieve, "Can I have that pattern when you're done? I'm about to be an aunt."

"Sure."

"Is Ralph out back?"

She nodded. "He's heating the coals. We'll be ready to cook in just a minute."

I excused myself, and went out the back door. Ralph stood by the huge Weber grill, one big enough to do a twenty pound turkey in. He looked over his little pyre obsessively. "Hello, and welcome to our humble abode."

"Nice house."

"Oh, Genevieve is itching to redecorate, but we don't have the money for it."

"You remember Peyton, don't you? I can recommend him highly as an interior designer who can decorate on a budget."

"So, how's your case going?"

"Oh, I don't know." I explained what had happened with Joe Canelli today, how that tied in with what Lynnette had told me. When I finished, I fell silent. Ralph watched me for a moment. Genevieve came out, setting a pile of steaks on the small table attached to the grill.

After she went back inside, Ralph said, "Now you used to work at Nouveau Deli before, right?"

I nodded.

"Close your eyes for a minute, and think about the delicatessen, then tell me what you're thinking."

"Hell hole." I didn't even need to close my eyes for that one.

"Hell hole?"

"Yeah." I felt the pain welling in my chest again. I pressed on it to make it feel better.

"Now, why is that?"

"Too much to do for too little money. Overworked and underpaid. God, I hated it. Hate it. I'd risen as far as I was going to go in less than a year. I couldn't figure out why I'd stayed as long as I did. Did I ever tell you about the day I quit?"

He shook his head.

"It was a Friday, and I had ten pick-up orders that had more than thirty sandwiches each. The sandwich makers weren't getting all the sandwiches made in time, and they were forgetting a lot of them. Jen and I tried as best we could to keep the angry customers from revolting.

"I decided to call Charlie to get some help, and he out and out refused. So I quit."

"Charlie. The guy who died."

"Yeah, the man who died. Murdered. You know, sometimes I'm surprised that I wasn't the person who killed him."

Ralph watched my outburst with interest in his eyes, but without comment. I felt embarrassed, and stopped speaking. I'd had no reason to ramble on uncontrollably about my hatred for work there. A simple question had brought it on.

Then, just as suddenly as my tirade began, my embarrassment faded. "Oh! Now I'm beginning to understand!"

CHAPTER 31
"Closing In"

I finally thought I knew the reason behind the food poisoning. It had literally stared me in the face since about day two, but it had taken me awhile to sift it out. I had touched on it before, but hadn't followed through on the hunch.

It wasn't Sid, not Lynnette. I was pretty sure it wasn't Joe Canelli, even if his background was a bit shady. No, I was fairly certain it was an employee, someone as angry as I was, getting back at management for being mistreated. Probably someone who'd worked at Nouveau Deli for at least a few years, someone who knew there was no management position in the future for him or her.

Because of the coincidence between when Ned Beyers was promoted and when the food loss started, I believed it was someone who'd interviewed for the kitchen manager's position. Someone who'd been there longer than Ned, and had gotten passed over. I had to get the list of interviewees from Sid. And fast.

This was what I thought of as I rode back from Ralph and Genevieve's house. The twilight weather at ten o'clock was cool and refreshing after the heat of the day. A breeze had picked up, playing with my hair as I biked along. The sky was clear, the stars peeking out from their blue hideaway, a sliver of moon in the sky. Perfect pondering weather.

Peyton was hammering away when I got home. I left him to his work for the time being, and went to the phone. I looked up Sid's new number and dialed. It rang twelve times before I hung up. I looked up Lynnette's number, and dialed again. She answered on the fourth ring.

"Hello."

"Hi, Lynnette? This is d'Arcy."

"What do you want?"

"Do you know where Sid is?"

"It's ten o'clock."

"It's important."

"I don't know. Am I his keeper?"

I wanted to say, 'you might be,' but I held my tongue. Instead, I said, "Well, do you happen to know who interviewed for the kitchen manager's job?"

She hung up without answering. Big help she was. On an off chance, I called Nouveau Deli. Jennifer picked up.

"Hello, Nouveau Deli, may I help you?"

"Hi, Jen, it's d'Arcy."

"Oh, d'Arcy. Just who I needed to talk to. Mack's grandmother died, and he was closing cashier tomorrow. I know you hate close, but can you fill in for him?"

The last thing I wanted to do. Yet another delay in my investigation. Or maybe not. "Sure, no problem," I said, instantly regretting it. "Is Sid in?"

"You're a lifesaver. Let me check, okay? May I put you on hold?"

"Sure." The hammering above my head had stopped, and now I could hear a chain saw going back and forth. "Hi, Peyton," I yelled, during one of the pauses.

"Oh, you're back," came the muffled reply.

"This is Sid," the phone said.

"Hi, d'Arcy here. Do you have a list of people who interviewed for kitchen manager?"

"Oh, I'm sorry. I forgot you wanted that. Hold on, I'll get it." Sid didn't put me on hold. He clunked the receiver onto the desk, and I listened an interminably long time while he searched through some paperwork. I could hear the muffled rustling. "Ah, here it is. Let's see. Ned, of course, who got it. Also, two people from nearby delis, including I may add, Joe's Cafe. Want their names?"

"No."

"No?"

"No. Go on."

"Well, Jennifer Lindsay, Cecille Brown, Richard Clark from sandwich making, and Patty deLaney from meats and cheeses."

I wrote down all the names, circling Cille and Jen. "Thanks, Sid. See you tomorrow."

"Save me soon. The health department geeks are all over my ass."

"Soon, Sid, soon. I'm getting really close." I hung up as Peyton opened the door from the attic.

"Come on up," he said, twanging a southern drawl. "You ain't gonna believe this."

"Stop with the southern bit, Peyton."

"Little high and mighty old thing, aren't you?" He winked, then turned and headed back upstairs. I followed. Reaching the top of the steps, I turned and gasped. Not only had Peyton removed the panelling from the entire back wall, pulled up the flooring where my bed and my bathroom would go, and double joisted those areas so they could take the extra weight, but he'd also replaced the floor with new plywood and cleared away the rest of the trashed lumber.

"Holy cow, Peyton, when did you do all this? What else is there to do?"

He smiled a big smile. "Barbra knows someone, a brother, I think, who's a contractor. She's going to try to get us a deal for hinging the roof. He might be able to do it this week."

"That's great. We're well on our way to an upstairs, aren't we?"

*   *   *

Much as I didn't want to believe it, I was afraid Jennifer was my woman behind the trouble at the deli. Richard Clark and Patty deLaney were both brand new supervisors. They'd worked at Nouveau Deli six or eight months at most, certainly not long enough to have developed a grudge. Besides, if anyone saw them carrying around a salad pan, they'd wonder why. Their departments had nothing to do with that salad case.

But Cille and Jennifer had been at the restaurant almost six and four years respectively. Of the two, Cille hadn't really shown interest in management before. In fact, she'd told me once, "I'm not management material, d'Arcy. I prefer the line. I don't have any desire to do that much paperwork, and I don't want to get away from working with the customers." I personally was even surprised she'd tried out for the kitchen position at all.

Jennifer, on the other hand, was ambitious and aggressive. She'd probably think after four years that a management position was her due, and it would look good on an eventual resume should she ever wish to leave. If she didn't get kitchen manager, but Ned had, she'd have been understandably pissed. Maybe the food poisoning incidents were meant to be a warning, and she hadn't intentionally meant to kill anyone.

That's what I wanted to believe, at least.

*   *   *

I got a phone call right before I left for work. Peyton answered it, and called me to the phone, not telling me who was on the other end. He grinned as I picked up the receiver. I knew something was up.

"D'Arcy speaking," I said.

"Hi, d'Arcy."

I should have known. Tim. I felt a chill of anxiety go down my back as I recognized his voice.

"How are you?" I asked, keeping my voice as cool as possible. He couldn't hear the hurt in my voice. I wouldn't let him. But I wanted him to hear my pain, too, in the paradoxical way I had with my emotions.

"Good. I wanted to ask you the same question."

"I'm okay. I might be wrapping this case up tonight, I hope."

"Oh, you're working?"

"Yeah. Got called in for close."

"Too bad. Well, what about after? When do you get off?"

"I don't think so."

"D'Arcy, what the hell did I do? Why are you so down on me all of a sudden?"

I looked at Peyton. I could tell by the way he looked at me he could hear Tim on the other end. He mouthed the words, "Tell him."

I took a deep breath. "Tim, you made me feel like a fool. I thought I got this job by myself, you know, because Ralph thought I deserved the chance. Maybe he thought I'd be good at it. Then I find out you got the job for me."

"I what?"

"That's what it sounded like to me."

"Oh, d'Arcy." Tim sighed. "I guess I can see how you got that impression. But that wasn't how it worked. See, Ralph was over at FitzRandolph and Roy, desperate because he needed another investigator. Asked if we knew any who might be interested in hooking up with him. I happened to mention that you weren't a licensed investigator, but you'd shown some natural ability up in Grayling. You should've seen his face. He said, "Jesus, God, I just set up an appointment with her. You see, you'd already done the legwork."

"Oh."

"Do you forgive me?"

I swallowed the lump in my throat. "Yeah. Sorry."

"So, I ask again, what time do you get off work tonight?"

I looked down at my watch, then wondered why I'd done that. God, d'Arcy, you are such an idiot. "Hard to say. Late. Ten? Ten thirty?"

"How about I pick you up? Maybe we could go out for drinks—"

"No, not drinks," I said, a bit too quickly. I chewed my bottom lip. I could hear Peyton laughing behind me, and I shot him a look to tell him to shut the fuck up.

Tim laughed. "Okay, dancing, maybe?"

"I'll be tired." Peyton literally kicked me in the butt. "Pizza?"

I pictured the two of us, almost exactly a month ago, sharing pizza in Grayling, Michigan. During more innocent times when we were asking what each other's hobbies were. "Pizza. Okay. Yeah, that sounds like a good idea. You'll pick me up?"

"Sure. Nouveau Deli, ten or so. Thanks, d'Arcy."

"No, thank you."

I hung up the phone, aware of the heartbeat pounding in my ears. I turned around. Peyton gave me a thumbs up. I grinned, feeling better than I had in days.

I made it to work by 1:30, even though I wasn't scheduled until two. Taking advantage of a surprising crowd of people there for a Monday afternoon, I went to the pop machine, poured myself a Diet Coke, then proceeded to intentionally drop it onto the floor.

Kneeling with the bleach rag in my hands, I cleaned up the mess I'd made. While I was at it, I had a good view of the underside of the refrigerated case where I'd last seen a rotting salad.

I wasn't too surprised to spot another salad pan, basking in the heat of the refrigerator exhaust. Apparently, my food poisoning friend had not been deterred by Charlie's death, nor by Cecille's food poisoning experience. Playing with fire, I had to say.

I checked who was on the line. Jennifer and Cille were standing together, talking. I assumed one was checking in with the other. I didn't know who was night supervisor and who was day supervisor. Another worker, Hank, was there, too, working one of the cash stands and taking a few orders.

I realized, once I'd cleaned up my Diet Coke and changed rags in the bleach bucket, that in spite of the people in the deli, there was not much business going on. Looking more carefully, I noticed at least three health inspectors I'd met last week.

They literally swarmed around the restaurant. The woman sat at a table. One of the men watched the salad line, while the other kept watch over the sandwich production area. Good. I'd probably need them later.

Judging by what I saw on further investigation, yet another man watched by the coffee machine, a woman stood by the kitchen, yet another few by each door. With all these eyes, how had the culprit planted the salad?

Very carefully.

I sidled up to one of the guys, near the pop fountain, and said, "Hey, I think I've got a break in this case."

He looked at me, confused. "Is it leaking?"

"What? Oh, no, not the pop machine. I mean, I found a salad under the salad case, it's gonna go into the case any time. Can you keep a watch out for anyone who seems to be fooling around under there?"

His eyes narrowed. "I don't know about all this."

"Look, I mean it. Keep an eye out, okay?"

He shrugged his shoulders. I didn't know how to convince him I was telling the truth, and right now I didn't have time. I had to get my cash drawer and be on line in a few minutes.

One commotion occurred just before I punched in. Ned came out, and stopped Jennifer on her way to the kitchen area.

"When are you going to add salads to your case?"

"I'm just doing it now."

"Why are you so late?"

"I'm not late, I'm right on time."

"Don't give me that crap. I've got a ton of salads wait-ing. You'll never get them out in time—"

"If you'd gotten them done before the lunch rush started, maybe you wouldn't have a pile up now. And there's nothing stopping you from bringing out a salad once it's made. Ever think maybe we were busy out here?"

"What are you insinuating? That I don't know my job?"

"Take it as it lays, Ned."

"I know my job, God damn it."

Jennifer pushed her way past him and went into the kitchen. Ned's face was bright red; he looked ready to pound her into the ground. Jennifer's face remained relatively placid, save for the fact that her eyebrow twitched and I saw her nos-trils flair.

But I knew what that meant. As soon as Jennifer got off shift, she'd go outside and cry. Having watched the scene, I had felt my blood pressure rise magically. The space between my breasts ached with stress.

I would figure out who was doing this today if it killed me. I wanted out of Nouveau Deli so bad, I could taste it.

CHAPTER 32
"A Cut Above"

Cille was the supervisor for the night time shift, I discovered when I came back from the office with my counted cash drawer. I waved to her as I set the cash pockets into the drawer and rang up the next customer. "Hey, Cille, one of the rifles I have is a Winchester 1886 Carbine. Do you want it?"

"Maybe, how much?"

"The antiques dealer says it's worth five grand."

"Yeah, that sounds about right. I'll have to see if I have the money for it."

"Well, let me know."

I was out of quarters, which was fine by me. I took another roll from my envelope, broke it on the side of the drawer, then deliberately let the roll fall to the ground. "Oh, damn," I said. "Cille, watch my drawer for a minute, would you? I dropped some quarters."

She looked over. "What's the matter with you, today? Got a case of the drops?"

"Yeah, I guess I do. I'll be okay in a minute." I dropped to my knees and scooped up the quarters. Above me, I could hear Cille ringing up each person in the line. Between those customers, she waited on people who wanted to place sandwich orders.

By far the most efficient line person at the deli. It was a job she was past being good at; she was the role model. And she had never asked to be manager, not once in six years. Except for this kitchen manager position. Why had she changed her mind?

When I finished picking up quarters I could see, I knelt farther, looking under the refrigerator case for any that had fallen there. The salad pan was gone.

During the ten minutes I'd counted my drawer in the back room, the salad pan had been slipped into the case.

I stood up and exchanged places with Cille, throwing my quarters into their respective bin. I rang up the next couple of customers, but my mind was not on that job. Jennifer was supervisor for morning shift, Cille for the afternoon.

Either of them had the same motive, the same opportunity. Which one, Cille or Jennifer, had wanted the kitchen manager position enough to kill for it?

Jennifer could have done it, knowing that when the shift change occurred, the blame would switch to Cille. Or to me.

But Cille was supposed to taste-test every salad at the beginning of her shift. Had she caught the bad salad? Or had it been put in after she tasted them all? By whom?

I was the one at a disadvantage. I didn't know which salad in the case was the tainted one. And I didn't want any more deaths by potato salad. How could I find out which one it was before I accidentally poisoned a customer with it?

"Excuse me. Are you going to ring me up or not?" A woman stood in front of me, her cheeks turning red in the afternoon sun which streamed in behind me.

"I'm so sorry," I said, and rang up her order. "$26.05, please."

"God, the service in this place has gotten worse and worse. And the prices just keep rising."

I took her money, not replying. I could feel Cille's glare as she watched me, telling me without saying a word that treating customers poorly was a fatal error at Nouveau Deli. One I could lose my job over. Ha. Please, please, you couldn't make me happier.

At my break, I looked for the Health Department officials again. If I could get their attention and let them know there was a bad salad in the case, maybe they could help me.

I searched with no avail. They'd been swarming around for hours. Now that I needed them, they'd disappeared on me. Great, just great.

At my break, I tried to call Hughes Investigations. There was no answer. Damn. Where was Genevieve? I hadn't brought their home phone number with me, and I couldn't remember it off the top of my head.

As I hung up, I could feel a silly sense of panic rising in my chest, but I tried to will it back down. I wanted help, but couldn't get it. I'd have to think of some alternative.

Finally, I took my place back at the register. "The place has cleared out a bit, huh?" I said to Cille, hoping I didn't let on my fear.

"Yeah, the Health Department vultures have left for the day," Cille said. "But we'll be back early tomorrow," she said, changing her voice to indicate she was imitating one of them.

I nodded, my heart sinking. The guy from the Health Department hadn't believed me. Now there was no one here but me to sort this out.

CHAPTER 33
"Dressing for Murder"

Cille had a break. Then she let Hank eat. At six p.m., dinner rush began.

And a legitimate rush it was. Must have been a Detroit Tigers game at home, because huge amounts of kids and fathers lined up to order sandwiches. The Tigers, after all, had been doing well for the first time in a long time.

Pick up order business was also brisk. I had my hands full trying to wrap sandwiches and ring up all my customers without slowing my line down too much.

When I could, I helped take orders. By some blessed coincidence, no one I personally waited on wanted anything in the salad case. I didn't know which salad to steer them away from. But what was happening on Cille's end?

Finally, around seven thirty, the crowd thinned. Cille began spooning salads from this day's pans into clean new pans from the kitchen, to prepare for the morning shift. I helped her when I could, going back and forth to the dishwashing area to take back dirty pans and pick up more clean ones.

One time, I returned in time to overhear Cille talking with a customer who'd come up during my absence. "Oh, you know, I really don't care for that particular salad," she told them. "I don't like the ham we use for that one. It's from Arkansas. Why don't you try the ham and pea salad instead? That's Virginia ham, much better tasting."

I rang up my next customer as I watched Cille spoon out a bit of salad for her customer to taste. I didn't make any conversation. Ham and pea salad. She had purposely steered a customer away from one salad and toward that one. Why?

And what was this about not liking the ham we used? Cille loved Arkansas ham; in fact, she loved any kind of ham. What was she doing? Steering a customer toward a salad to poison him? Or to keep from poisoning the customer?

So maybe that was why there'd been no customer food-poisoning. . .

That idea put a lot of perspective on what had been happening all along. Cille had steered that customer toward a salad that had not been sitting under the refrigerator all day.

She knew which salad it was.

I peered into the case to see what other salads we had. Salmon salad, ham and potato salad. Could be that one. It had poisoned Charlie. But then, it also had Virginia ham in it, said so right on the sign.

Would a customer be foolish enough not to pick up on Cille's lie there?

Going on, we had two all vegetable salads, a vegetarian potato salad, pasta carbonara salad, old fashioned ham and pea salad—

Back it up, I thought as I hurried to ring up another customer. The pasta carbonara salad. We used Arkansas ham in that one instead of the customary bacon. Was that the salad?

At nine o'clock, the deli closed. I needed to count my cash drawer and leave funds in for the next morning. Then I'd help Cille clean the three cases.

The sandwich production staff finished up early and clocked out. Then the kitchen people went. That left Cille and me to finish up. I thought I even saw Sid, the night manager, leave.

After I'd finished my drawer, I said, "God, I'm hungry. Cille, do you think I could serve myself a side of something and you ring it up on the other drawer before I finish it out?"

She didn't answer. She was busily pulling spoons and rinsing them in the sink below the case. I opened the door and leaned in. I was hit by an unmistakable sulphur smell. Rotting eggs. "Cille, there's—"

I pulled my head out of the case to look at her. That's when I noticed the butcher knife in her hand. "Don't move," she said.

"Cille, what are you doing?"

"Don't play coy with me. I know you know. I suspected it when you spilled your pop this afternoon."

"What are you trying to do?"

She stepped toward me, the knife flashing as she raised it toward my neck. "You were always the chosen one, you know. Little Princeton grad, you and Ned were the prized finds. You left before Ned and you could fight to see who'd get a manager spot first. But the next management position is mine, not yours."

"I never wanted to be a manager here."

"Sure you didn't. Everyone wants manager. I want manager, but I've never said that to anyone." She hesitated, lowering the knife slightly. "So why did you come back, then?"

"To investigate an alleged food poisoning problem."

"Alleged. You and your fancy terms. It was an honest to God goddamn food loss problem." She laughed, raised her knife again and came closer to my neck. I stepped back a few paces, moving from our refrigerator cases to the small meat and cheese case beyond the second register. I could hear the whirring of the meat slicer behind me; Cille must have turned it on to clean it. I stepped away from the counter to avoid it.

"But you always said you didn't want a management position," I said.

"And there's no Santa Claus, either, Virginia. I was lying, waiting for the perfect job. Kitchen manager was it. I wouldn't have to deal with the customers then. Didn't I tell you not to move?"

I stopped my backward movement. I'd reached the wall anyway. There was no other place to go. "So, when Ned was chosen to be kitchen manager, you started leaving salads out so they would spoil. Didn't you?"

"It's so damn easy. But it didn't go according to plan. All I wanted was for someone to notice, and fire Ned for incompetence."

"You steered a customer away from a tainted salad today, didn't you? Are you trying to frame Ned?"

"No guests will ever get hurt."

"Instead, you killed Charlie with your stupid plan."

"Don't call it stupid, it'll work, I promise you," she yelled, lunging suddenly. I thought she was going to go for my neck, so I tucked and moved to the right. Instead, she'd gone left, nearly falling on the slick floor. "It should have worked already."

"You didn't expect Sid to hire an undercover investigator, did you? He hired me again, to find out why the food poisonings were occurring."

"You're not an investigator."

"I am."

For a moment, she looked shocked. Then her lips curled into a sickening smile. "I should have known you hadn't come back by your own free will."

"You just said I came back to get a manager position. Make up your mind."

"Shut up, you bitch! Shut up. Maybe you were the one who killed Charlie. You were supervisor that day. You poisoned me."

"You were working, too. Why didn't you stop him from eating that salad?" A sudden thought dawned on me, as illogically as her thoughts were tumbling out into the conversation. I said, "Wait, did you rig the flourescent tube to fall, too?"

"I rigged nothing. You were the one. You poisoned Charlie. You poisoned me. You broke the tombstone attachment so the flourescent tube would fall."

I couldn't tell if she'd gone totally nuts on me, convincing herself I really had done it, or if she was trying to decide her alibi for why she had to kill me now. And this was a woman I'd just offered to sell a rifle to. Before I knew.

I had to get her knife before she cut one or the other of us. But how?

"You forgot about Ben Mitchell."

She straightened. "Who?"

"Lynnette's lover. You killed him, too."

"I don't know what you're talking about."

I lunged for her. She apparently didn't notice until too late, because the knife fell out of her hands as I hit her, and it clattered to the floor. I grabbed both of her hands in vice grips.

Then I slipped on the wet floor. It was then that I realized how close we both were to the slicer. Somehow I had to turn it off.

I let go of her left hand and reached the switch. Snap. I'd turned off the power. Just then, she hit my arm, knocking it upward. It took me a moment to control its flight. Then I reached up, grabbing for her wrist again. That's when I noticed the blood.

My own blood. My mind seemed to disembody itself as I looked back at the slicer, smeared a quarter of an inch deep with my blood. My arm was covered. I couldn't tell where the cut started or ended. Had I sliced an artery? I felt no pain.

With sudden fury, I attacked Cille. I grabbed a hank of her hair, and then I fell, suddenly devoid of energy. She fell with me, on top of me.

Cranbrook-Kingswood, eighth grade, a classmate making fun of me because I'd just started my period. I had screamed at my own blood. And when she smirked and cat-called and told me she'd had hers for three years already, we started to fight. I clawed her hair, she scratched my cheeks with her nails. But I won the fight. I hadn't let myself down.

I thought I heard sirens. But they were a long, long way off. Or had I heard the knocking first? Was that my head? I saw faces. Cille's, frozen with pain and horror. Tim Reams behind her, I thought, but I couldn't tell. Maybe it was a dream. Sid.

My fingers carefully being unclenched from Cille's hair. Then complete, quenching blackness.

CHAPTER 34
"All Wrapped Up"

A weak beeping sound intruded my sleep. Did it keep time with the dull thudding in my head, or just echo it? I tried to open my eyes, but someone had pasted them shut.

I dreamed, then, a dream about my father. He picked me up and took me to a daisy strewn shore, where he placed me on the banks of a mighty river. He said, "This is your destiny. Try to accept your past. It will serve you well." Then he led me to the back seat of a canoe, gave me one paddle, and waved as I set off.

I groaned. I didn't get it. What did he mean? Why had I dreamed of him, of all people? One of two people who loved me the least.

I woke up to bright white sheets and a green ceiling. I surveyed my surroundings, and found my father, sitting to my right.

"Father?"

"Ssh, honey, I'm here."

"What the hell—" I tried to sit up, but felt a sharp pain down my left arm, and decided I didn't have the energy to move.

"You're in the hospital, but you're going to be all right. It's a good hospital, I promise you."

He had made sure I was in a good hospital. Typical. Where else would he have his only daughter go? "You were in my dream."

"I was?"

"Where's mother?"

"She's resting. We've been taking turns watching you."

Must have been a bad accident if both Mother and Father were here. My eyes continued to scan the room. That was when I found Tim sleeping in another chair, to my left.

"He's been here the whole time, refuses to leave," my father said. "He was the one who saved you."

It all came back to me then. Cille attacking me, the slicer. I felt faint for a moment, just remembering my blood as it covered my arm and clothes.

Tim had said he'd meet me at the deli. He must have arrived early and seen us fighting through the window.

"You went into shock. They were afraid they wouldn't bring you around." My father touched my forehead; his fingers felt warm. "Well, now that you're awake and okay, I think I'll gather up your mom and we'll be going. I know you don't believe it sometimes, but we love you very much."

He squeezed my hand and kissed my forehead, then left. When I turned back to Tim, I realized he'd awakened.

"Hi, sleepyhead," I said.

"Oh, d'Arcy, God, I was so worried about you."

"What happened to Cille?"

"She's in prison, waiting for them to post bail. But from what I hear, she won't be let out at all. There's a special place for her in the psychiatric hospital."

"Oh, you mean she'll be living down the street from me?" I laughed, but I could tell Tim had no idea what I was talking about. "You know, the County Hospital just down Michigan

Avenue from me."

"Oh, I get it."

We were silent for a few minutes. I watched him twist the class ring on his right hand. I felt like I was about to go to sleep, but I didn't want to.

"You must have arrived just in time."

"I saw you in the window. It took a second to see the knife. The door was locked, I began beating on the door about the time she dropped it. But not soon enough to keep you from getting cut. Sid came running toward me. He was the night manager, I guess, and he'd just stepped out for a few minutes, to get more bleach, he said. He called 911 after he let me in."

He squeezed my hand, then held it up to show me the bandage. It covered my entire forearm, from elbow to wrist. "Pretty spectacular, huh? Seventy two stitches. The doctor says the amount of muscle you had saved you. You missed a main artery by a fraction, your muscles were in the way."

"Will I be able to bodybuild again?"

"Oh, sure, but you'll have to take off a few weeks until the cut heals."

Tim said something else, but I didn't hear him. Instead, I heard the ocean, coming in in waves, surrounding my head like cool, salty tears.

I was back home the next day. Peyton made me oatmeal for lunch, since that was all I felt like eating. It tasted good, though. He mixed it with melted cheddar cheese and milk, to give me some protein.

Around 1:30, Sid came by. "How's the patient?" he asked when Peyton let him in.

"So so."

He handed me a check for three thousand dollars.

"Well, feeling much better now, thank you," I said. I looked at the check and when I realized how much it was for, I added, "But this is way too much."

"No, it's not. You helped me out of a bind, and did it in a little over a week. You don't know how much it means to me.

I figured I owed you some workers' comp, too. Besides, did you hear?"

"Hear what?"

"My business has been incredible since the news release about you. Lynnette's decided to sell her half of the deli to me."

"Is that good news?"

"Good enough. And I took what you said about the salary discrimination to heart. I'm going to make sure women make as much as the men do. Now, any chance I can convince you to come back? I've got a plum management position open right now that could be yours. You'd, uh, you'd start at fifty grand."

Peyton sucked in his cheeks.

I laughed. "Never, Sid. No offense."

"Oh, well, maybe Jennifer will accept the job."

"She deserves it, Sid."

He left soon after, saying, "Come by and visit some time, I'll give you a free sandwich."

Peyton came into the room with a cup of coffee for me. "So, how's the patient?"

"Everyone keeps saying that."

"We care."

"Right."

He wrapped the afghan around me. "We do. By the way, which rifles are we selling, again?"

"All except the two best ones."

"What are you keeping them for?"

"You take the Browning. The other I might give to my father."

Peyton acted as if he hadn't heard. I told him again. He didn't have to say anything. The big grin on his face told me he was happy with his present. "Does your father like rifles?"

"Hell if I know. That's not really the point. He never bought me anything I really wanted."

The doorbell rang. Peyton went to answer it. Standing there, hidden by a dozen peach colored roses, was Tim.

About the Author

CHRISTINE COOK lives in Ann Arbor, Michigan, with her husband, two children and Oscar the Masked Cat. She is currently working on the next novel in the d'Arcy W. Carter series. In addition to mysteries, she also writes childrens' books.

Quick Order Form

Postal Orders:
    Porch Swing Press
    2258 Courtney Circle Court
    Ann Arbor, Michigan 48103
    U.S.A.
    Telephone: (734) 213-1370

Please send me _____ books at $9.95 each $ _____

Michigan residents please add 6% sales tax $ _____

Shipping:
U.S. Shipping: $4.00 for first book;
        $2.00 each additional
(International Shipping: $9.00 for first
        book; $5.00 each additional): $ _____

Check enclosed for this amount: $ _____

Ship to:
Name: _____
Address: _____
Address 2: _____
City: _____
State: _____ Zip Code: _____

NOTE: Ordering questions, call (734) 516-1370.
    Please allow 4-6 weeks for delivery.

Quick Order Form

Postal Orders:
     Porch Swing Press
     2258 Courtney Circle Court
     Ann Arbor, Michigan 48103
     U.S.A.
     Telephone: (734) 213-1370

Please send me _____ books at $9.95 each $ _____

Michigan residents please add 6% sales tax $ _____

Shipping:
U.S. Shipping: $4.00 for first book;
     $2.00 each additional
(International Shipping: $9.00 for first
     book; $5.00 each additional): $ _____

Check enclosed for this amount: $ _____

Ship to:
Name: _____
Address: _____
Address 2: _____
City: _____
State: _____ Zip Code: _____

NOTE: Ordering questions, call (734) 516-1370.
    Please allow 4-6 weeks for delivery.